THE SNOW BALL

BRIGID BROPHY

THE SNOW BALL

faber

This edition first published in 2020
by Faber & Faber Ltd
Bloomsbury House, 74–77 Great Russell Street
London WC1B 3DA

Typeset by Faber & Faber Limited
Printed in the UK by CPI Group (UK) Ltd, Croydon CR0 4YY

A CIP record for this book
is available from the British Library

ISBN 978–0–571–36287–5

FOREWORD

by Eley Williams

'*What* a mood. What a *mood*,' said Anne.

And here is the invitation to Brigid Brophy's dazzling *The Snow Ball*, a feminist remodelling of libertine fervour and passion by one of the great prose stylists of the twentieth century. I use the word *dazzling* advisedly as, in many ways, *The Snow Ball* centres upon that very concept: the allure of dazzlement, states of enthralment or rapture, and the potent vulnerability of the dazed.

'In a sense, the first (if not necessarily the prime) function of a novelist, of *any* artist, is to entertain.' The continuation of this line from Brophy's provocative *Fifty Works of English Literature We Could Do Without* (1967) reveals what might be valued most highly about her own work: 'If the poem, painting, play or novel does not immediately engage one's surface interest then it has failed. Whatever else it may or may not be, art is also entertainment. Bad art fails to entertain. Good art does something in addition.' *The Snow Ball* certainly passes this test, for while the pomp, swing and swagger of her novel do wholly *entertain*, they also prompt the reader to consider the effects and affects of pleasure and diversion. The book could be described as a sprightly comedy of manners, but it is never 'merely' that. It is a witty riffing on the repertoires of seduction, *and* an exhibition and critique of sumptuousness and desire; it is an elegant meditation on sexuality and psychology, *and* a camp refiguring of canons of Western art. Wry, stylish, philosophical: all this, and that, and more, while bright white peppermints rain down upon characters' heads, their fingertips extended in poses of ecstasy and with powdered wigs falling askew.

As the curtain rises and the novel begins, we find ourselves in the throes of a costumed party on New Year's Eve. While the setting for the novel is a recognisably modern world of tutting taxi drivers and 'monstrous electric' fires, characters don eighteenth-century glamour and clamour and costumery in the rooms of a fancy, ornate house. It is a moment of commotion and suspension, thematically and dramatically. It is here that protagonist Anna K considers the opportunity (or is it a burden?) to swap convention for confection and to enter into a performance of seductions, coveted illicit affairs and flights of fantasy. Characters are shown to be alert to their own and others' nuances and complexities ('for a few seconds there was a contest of narcissisms') as well as their protracted performances made for the sake of others, alongside more private, protective, 'dispassionate' artifices: it is a world where carefully chosen masks slip, breeches must be readjusted and beauty spots are studiously applied and discarded to achieve different effects. The result is a novel written with frisson and release about perusal and pursuit. *The Snow Ball* traces characters who seek to communicate with one another as quarries or trackers, lovers or friends, and Brophy both revels in and skewers their abilities to express themselves through aspect or dialogue, via chronicles kept secretly in shorthand diaries or in hasty notes passed hand to hand. Courtship and companionship, queer rivalry and attraction, imposition and sensuality are all Brophy's material. There is flirtatious dialogue and the thrusts and parries of intellectual one-upmanship; and even an impish portrait of the horrors of mansplaining in the guise of the marvellously named Dr Brompius, deliverer of pompous bromides, who is forever lurking in the wings.

Although the novel uses the events and associative evocative moods of Mozart's *Don Giovanni* as its backdrop and informing pattern, it is not necessary for one to have a detailed knowledge of the opera. The pleasure of reading *The Snow Ball*, with its heady mixture of mischievous delight and antic indulgence, recalls Wayne Koestenbaum's description of listening to opera recordings when alone: 'The banquet for one . . . I feel I am locked in the bathroom eating a quart of ice cream, that I have lost all my friends, that I am committing some violently antisocial act, like wearing lipstick to school.' Possibly more important than any specific comparisons to *Don Giovanni*'s plot or narrative,

Brophy's novel emphasises elements of experiencing an opera that extend beyond its story, such as staging, volume and theatricality, and how they might be enacted through fiction. *The Snow Ball* is full of references to artfulness in an array of different media alongside textual depiction or description, and the reader is often treated as someone privy to notes by a director or wardrobe consultant rather than as a passive audience member: the narrator imagines 'a film camera taking it all in', sweeping through parts of the novel and permitting multiple viewpoints, granting access to a sweeping, bustling dramaturgy of a scene as well as the ability to zoom in on tiny details to catch characters' telling tics and idiosyncrasies. Elsewhere the reader is urged to 'judge' with the narrator – 'how little sense of period; how overdone' – and also to consider the addition of a soundtrack 'mounted' upon a character's consciousness. Brophy's novel is about artificiality, about coded gesture and performance, and it is entirely appropriate that it draws attention to itself as a site of crafted world-making in which the reader can take part.

It is a deeply funny book, where characters are shown committing and committed to revelry, and Brophy is unafraid to include giggles and laughter that – like the words 'foam' and 'frills' – repeat as refrains throughout the novel. The pursuit of levity and satiating of appetites shapes *The Snow Ball*, but it is also concerned with ageing and agency, disrepair and decadence, as much as it is with frenetic, fraught, sought-after passion. Again, an emphasis falls upon artifice linked with a particular rococo spirit. Just as the psychologies and actions of its dilettante and stoic characters can be read as studies of illusion, excess and melodrama, this is mirrored in their surroundings, where stucco putti exist as a combination of finery and kitsch grotesqueries (where statues have 'rouged buttocks for cheeks'; 'in fresco, the babies had the sugariness of meringues'). The rococo decoration extends to linguistic sophistication and even to the shape of words, which take on the significance of baroque ornamentation: words as frescoes, carefully wrought in sentences such as 'the walls' plumbness she had turned into plumpness', so that the *trompe l'oeil* of a dripping filigree or the swing of a New Year's Eve pendulum can be traced in the letter *b*'s transformation into a *p*.

Erotic and contemplative, raucous and deliberate, *The Snow Ball* is a triumph of imaginative flair and powerful insight. In terms of structure, texture, tone and milieu, the novel plays and positions explicit pleasures alongside the anxious dynamics of implication in a novel that is delighting and delightful. The crystalline and stucco, the poised and imbalanced: Brophy's art is fiction at its finest.

Suggested further reading:

Brigid Brophy, *Mozart the Dramatist: A New View of Mozart, His Operas and His Age* (1964).

Brigid Brophy, Michael Levey and Charles Osborne, *Fifty Works of English and American Literature We Could Do Without* (1967).

Brigid Brophy, *Prancing Novelist: A Defence of Fiction in the Form of a Critical Biography in Praise of Ronald Firbank* (1973).

Richard Canning and Gerri Kimber (ed.), *Brigid Brophy: Avant-Garde Writer, Critic, Activist* (2020).

Jonathan Gibbs, *The Large Door* (2019).

Wayne Koestenbaum, *The Queen's Throat: Opera, Homosexuality, and the Mystery of Desire* (1993).

Susan Sontag, *Notes on Camp* (1964).

To Charles Osborne

'That most fascinating subject for gossip, whether, when the opera opens, Don Giovanni has just seduced or has just failed to seduce Donna Anna, will no doubt go on being debated for another *two centuries*.'

Brigid Brophy: *Mozart The Dramatist*, footnote.

'atque hoc evenit in labore atque in dolere, ut mors obrepat interim.'

Plautus: *Pseudolus*, II, iii

PART ONE

PART ONE

1

The double doors at the end of the ballroom were thrust open. Some of the people into whose backs they were thrust resisted and resented for a moment and then, understanding, made way. A space was created and at the same time a pause, as though someone very important or very fat was about to enter and nothing of smaller weight could command attention meanwhile. At last a sedan chair was carried in at a run.

On its roof, which was black and probably tarred, stood a few flakes of snow.

Seeing them from above—she was standing in the minstrels' gallery—Anna held her breath in enchantment for as long as it took them to melt.

The sedan chair was grounded and people closed in, milling up to and about it, like snowflakes themselves, making it as difficult for the woman inside to get the door opened as if a snowdrift really had been compiling against it; and everyone was laughing in the invigorated way of people who had suddenly discovered that it had snowed.

One man was standing against the drift of the crowd, shewing no interest in the arrival of the sedan chair and evidently neither with nor looking for a party of his own. He had a large paunch which he carried behind a waistcoat of opalescent chinese silk, and to Anna's view he made the shape of a boiled egg, which she might have been looking down on at the breakfast table—a boiled egg in a neat little chinoiserie egg-cosy. He was holding, at shoulder height, a small cup of coffee, and his only concern was to protect it from the crush.

Anna's hand at her side gathered control over her long skirt. But she waited a moment more in the gallery. The woman in the sedan chair was still laughing through its window, deploring in mime her difficulty in opening not only the door but her fan, which she obviously wanted to use; her face was already flushed. The paunched man, meanwhile, deciding it was safer to move, tottered to the edge of the ballroom, where he found an empty place on a rout bench. Holding his coffee higher than ever—indeed, above his head—he slowly began to sit down. Just before sitting he made, with his free hand, a gesture of hitching his trousers and then remembered they were knee breeches.

Anna descended the grand staircase, knowing that Voltaire and Lady Hamilton were waiting for her in the crowd at the bottom. The noise, the scents, the very warmth of the people's skins came to her as unmistakably twentieth-century. A film camera taking it all in from her place in the minstrels' gallery would have captured not a moment's illusion. You would merely judge: What a *bad* costume piece; how little sense of period; how overdone.

She touched the back of Lady Hamilton's shoulder. 'Did you see the sedan chair?'

'No?' Lady Hamilton peered where Anna indicated, into the ballroom, whose matching double doors at this, the opposite end, had been open all the time. But on ground level it was impossible to see to the other end for people. Anna was afraid Lady Hamilton might deduce she had been looking down from above. Indeed, 'Where did you get to?' Lady Hamilton asked, but Anna was already saying:

'It had snow on its roof.'

'Must be snowing outside,' said Voltaire.

'Must be.'

'Must be.'

Over the heads of the men it might have been possible to see, because most men were lopped tonight, their stature cut off at the earliest moment short of scalping by close, severe wigs. But the women were correspondingly built high. Their piled hair suggested, without defining, a fetichists' ball, as though they were wearing high heels on their heads.

There were sounds of chairs and fiddle bows being scraped. Evidently the band—which was not using the minstrels' gallery because it would have been too cramped—had come back to its position on a shallow platform at one side of the ballroom.

'First snow of the year,' said Voltaire.

'Of whichever year.'

'O no,' he replied, looking on his wrist for his watch and then drawing it out of the pocket where he had lodged it for verisimilitude, 'it's not quite——'

A crowd movement from behind them lifted Anna away and set her down inside the ballroom, where people she did not know told her she must make up the set or she would spoil it, an admonition she did not understand until the band's scrapings turned into music of a Scottish cast.

She began jumping up and down on the spot, which was all they required of her for the moment.

It must, pace Voltaire, whose watch perhaps went slower in his pocket, be getting on for midnight. It must be the approach of midnight that was already colouring the music.

Anna could not remember the figures but she supposed someone would tell her when it was her turn to trip out to the centre: unless midnight should come first.

Once a year, the iron tongue of midnight spoke in a Scottish accent.

She was conscious not merely of looking but of being absurd in having joined in. At twenty she would have pouted and refused to be a sport.

'I *hate* new years,' said a man's voice, dancing past, putting a social and jocular face on a sentiment that was true.

The man opposite Anna, in the place corresponding

to hers in the opposite row, was wearing a kilt, a black velvet coat and a froth of white lace down his chest. He was short, and hollowed out by middle age; and his sporran leapt hectically, leapt breathlessly, up and down, not keeping time with the lighter leaps of his jabot.

Anna's absurdity was to do this with the face and the drinking habits of middle age. The neat whisky she had been drinking brought her heart not to her mouth but, much more discomfortably, to the flat part of her chest, to what seemed to be a precise location on top of the flat bone above the breasts.

Even the music, although, being traditional, it ought to have been timeless, seemed to her as unmistakably twentieth-century as the faces which were jumping up and down——jumping once in their own right and again in Anna's vision——and which betrayed the ball.

Someone's fingers pushed her, bruisingly, and she ran to the centre in order not to disappoint an unknown Pompadour who was already waiting at an empty rendezvous. Hands clasped high, they scurried round an imaginary maypole, never quite catching up with where they ought to have been according to the music. It was really they, high-haired, unused to the exercise, who were maypoles.

One of the things you would judge overdone was beauty spots. They might have drifted lavishly down on to the female faces in a black snowstorm.

Now two other women had to do it.

The consciousness of any one of these women must be indistinguishable from Anna's own: in every case a consciousness of exhaustion, ageing absurdity and the approach of another year. Everyone grew a year older at once on new year's eve, even those whose birthdays had been the day before. They gathered, Anna decided, for consolation: wearing historical costume to offset the advance of history.

Not the most careless costume piece would have submitted an ageing Marie Antoinette to the absurdity of tripping to her rendezvous and encountering another ageing Marie Antoinette.

Suppose to the camera's view from the gallery was added a soundtrack on which they had mounted Anna's consciousness. The camera would be hard put to it to know which of these women was she. It would have to descend, approach, enquire into faces; quiz this beauty spot; explore the flabby, jumping cheek flesh of that Marie Antoinette; insert its lens into the spring of corkscrew curl flapping above these temples. It would find itself sliding with a drunken coiffure here, slipping there with a shoulder strap; it would stumble and recover a heel: it would begin to dissolve in the melting heat: as it stooped to retrieve a glittering, tumbling, spiralling ear-ring, the jewels would lose translucence and its vision be swamped in a flurry of black beauty spots, unseated by sweat, drifting stormily to the floor . . .

However, she steadied herself by looking at the distant wall which she knew, though she could not see, was not jumping up and down; she managed to screw her earring on again, jarring the lobe of her ear as she jumped; and when her eyes shifted back to a closer focus she recognised that the man in Scottish costume dancing opposite her was Rudy Blumenbaum. 'Hullo. Who're you? Bonnie Prince Charlie?'

'Ti tum ti tum,' he called back and laughed loudly, even as he turned with his line and began to trot away from her. He was out of breath; she was deaf with the pulses in her ears.

'I can't hear.'

'Ti tum—'

She was swept with her line into a circle: a snake had made the decision to eat itself: she saw Rudy's Scottish shirt pass like a streak of white impasto laid across a sombre painting.

She thought she knew what everyone in the room was thinking. On new year's eve it was impossible not to think of the approach of death.

The circle straightened again. Rudy reappeared, unexpectedly close. '*Who* did you say you were?'

'I'm Rabbi Burns,' he shouted, dancing away from her again, leaving behind him a hoot of Scottish-Jewish laughter, a sound of owls, bagpipes and ritual lugubriousness.

As if in obedience to the association of ideas, the band

cut itself off, drew three lines on the strings beneath what it had done and after a formal, rolling prelude began to play Auld Lang Syne. Some of the dancers did not understand for a moment or could not stop. Even Anna, thankful to stop, was distressed to find herself in the wrong line, until she remembered that after midnight it did not matter. Her arms were painfully crossed in front of her body, appositely in the gesture of a martyr. Rudy on her right was clasping her left hand, painfully pumping it up and down and squeezing her wedding ring into her flesh by the pressure against it of his signet ring. A masked stranger in a black costume had her right hand. She was singing, without knowing the words, embarrassed to be singing in public: after the parody of ballet, the parody of opera. The song straggled noisily away. No one knew the words. People began kissing, celebrating or assuaging the stroke of the one midnight a year which changed everyone into Cinderella. Rudy had turned away from her to the woman on the other side of him. Anna remembered it was his wife. She looked away, and began to move away from the dance floor. The masked man in black costume began to kiss her, not socially but on the lips, gently and erotically, then with a voluptuous fluttering, and at last with a violent and passionate exploration.

When he let her go, she remained facing him, staring deep into the eye-slits of his mask. The mask had not been unsettled by the embrace.

8

'Who are you?'

'I'm Don Giovanni. Who are you?'

She continued looking intently at him, even though people were moving about now, kissing more promiscuously, blowing whistles, making up half-dancing, arm-locked, straggling lines of three or four.

'Who are you?' he repeated.

'I'm safe so long as I don't tell you.'

'Safe?'

A storm of balloons was loosed from the ceiling. A green one fell between her and Don Giovanni. Neither of them moved. It touched them both, bounced and slowly reached the ground. He put his index finger for a second to the bridge of his nose, to feel that the mask was still in place.

'I'm Donna Anna,' she said.

She put her hand up to the back of her head to re-secure the tall Spanish comb and the brief drift of black lace it held there. She had sewn a dozen sequins to the black lace; and as her hand touched it she heard or felt a tiny spattering of them come tumbling down.

2

Babies in baroque pictures and rococo decorations seemed to incarnate the pure, sweet, all-desirable prettiness of sugar. Painted, modelled, carved; profane putti or almost wholly profaned cherubs: it made no difference: and there were hundreds of them in this house . . . They swarmed in delicate flights over its ceilings and alighted wherever it offered them a plinth or a pinnacle; they were its genius.

A group of them, rather orange in colour, supported a cloud on an oval canvas inset, among the fruits of a plaster orchard, on the ceiling of the hall. One looked down, almost malevolent, from the edge of a soffit as you left the ballroom: unwary, you might look suddenly up and catch its evil eye. Three chased one another for a veiled purpose up the drawing room wall, fluttering round half a trompe l'oeil column: the whole, fragmented column and all but fragmented cupids—one of them lacked the last inch of fleeing heel—was a patch rescued, and transferred here, from a destroyed fresco.

In fresco, the babies had the sugariness of meringues, their bottoms whipped but only as white of egg was whipped and left, standing up stiff, in a spiralled dollop. They represented a confectioner's notion of a sea-urchin. Faint dustiness of surface suggested that a percussive finger could powder them away: and yet the minutely granular texture of their surface implied they were bound all through with the resilience of white of egg, actually bound together and bodied forth with indestructible bubbles of air. In other parts of the house they were made of stucco: or—like the big Cupid looking down the grand staircase—wood: or again, shrinking now in scale, porcelain. In porcelain they took on the alabaster half-translucence of sugar just touched by moisture. The half-translucence was a hint, like half-nudity: it hinted that something irresistibly desirable was just on the point of being dissolved on the tip of a tongue.

Yet everywhere, in every part of the house, when you looked at them in detail, they were hideous. Seen close to, their airiness was an airy carelessness: a flick from the carver's wrist, a clumsy squeeze from the moulder's thumb, a mere blob from a clogged brush.

They were utter little monsters.

Worse than earthy, they had rouged buttocks for cheeks; dots, blank or malicious, for eyes; and either a nose stuck on, an appliqué nose, protruding, not always even centrally, like a carnival beak or else no nose at all, a nose merely implied by the presence of one hideously large, dark, curling nostril.

Anna knew, without regret, that her face belonged to their category—which was, perhaps, why she felt the most welcome, the most fitting and fitted, of guests in this house. It was almost a sibling's salute she gave in passing to the monster Cupid in his niche above the grand staircase.

Her face did not preclude her from being an attractive woman, any more than theirs precluded decorative putti from being decorative. But it was, or it provoked, a question of taste, a question of style. Anyone who contemplated forming an intimate relation to this face must ask himself whether he possessed such a taste and, possessing it, was prepared to develop it. That would demand that he immerse his senses in it, undergoing a larger and larger dose of exposure to it, until he became in a way calloused. The face would yield sensuous pleasure: but the sensualist must undertake an ascetic self-discipline first. He must harden himself to tolerate a tragic face whose tragedy was couched in half-formed baby features which, individually smudged and then squeezed up close together, had finally slipped or been twisted sideways in relation to the face, making it the face of an immortal baroque baby pettishly carrying into middle age the impress of being newly, and distortingly, born.

Anna, whose own answer had long been Yes, she could tolerate it, cherished her face without pity or special pleading. She knew that to the eye of love its spoiled prettiness presented hints, minimal but recurrent, of the erotic, like the idea of an unfrocked nun. In the eye of self-love, the mirror, she had found its infinite rococo complexity infinitely interesting. A beautiful face might lead the mind that contemplated it into a daydream so unimpeded as to verge on sleep. Anna's face, like one of the lizards called monsters, would have startled you awake if you had been asleep to begin with, so grossly did it contradict every dream satisfaction: and yet it was to the imagination that it was addressed: it was as much a flight of fancy as a swag of putti supporting a cloud; the word it recurrently brought to mind was *fantastic*.

In particular, she was in sympathy with her face when she made it up. She sympathised with her reflexion not at all with a therapist's sympathy, the feeling that the handi-capped thing needed to be painstakingly built up before it could shew itself with even a semblance of equality among its fellows, but rather with the virtuoso craftsman's sym-pathy with the organic nature, the grain, the accidents that could be turned to account, of his medium. When she fled the dance floor, she made her excuse the disrepair that dancing and drink had wrought in her face. But that really was excuse, not cause. It was not the face fleeing to its repair, but Anna repairing to her favourite refuge:– com-munion, stimulation, re-creation, work to be done, all in relation to the reflexion of her face.

She could not seek that communion in the crowded room on the first floor which had been set aside for the women guests and where, in one of the pier glasses placed for the evening in two facing lines like the guard of honour at a wedding, she might have had to contemplate her face peeping vulgarly or surrealistically out from above someone else's bare shoulders. She went into the warmth, the smell of powder, the zoo chatter like the dropping and grinding together of nutshells on the floor, only for a moment, in order to retrieve the make-up case she had deposited there; and then pushed her way straight out again, between the warm bare backs like animals steaming in their stalls after a race, some of which, as she was recognised in the mirrors, responded to her passage like animal flesh responding to a palm it knew. Outside in the corridor she made her way through a further crowd, sparser, and less naked because it was composed of men as well as women. Having the advantage over the crowd of knowing the house, she rose over the crowd by mounting the second staircase, the one with deep steps, narrow treads and commonplace wood: up, stepping by layers out of the party noise as if it was a frilled petticoat: up, carrying her small rigid suitcase, as if going to a solitary picnic on the roof in the snow: up two floors, four flights—how rich one had to be in the twentieth century to sleep in the servants' quarters of an eighteenth-century house—to her hostess's bedroom.

She opened the door gently in case someone was in there: but the room was dark. She left it dark while she went in, lest light slopping out into the corridor should signal some guest, exploring or lost up here, that this was a room he might enter. Shutting the door cut short the last trace of party sound. Anna in the dark was muffled: in the central-heating warmth, so dry as to make it clear that no other human being was in the room; in the room's effect, which could be felt before it was seen, of quilting; and in the knowledge that this room always did receive her in.

She put on the light and the Siamese kitten in the middle of the white bed pricked up its head, shook it —so violently that its ears made in miniature the waxed creaking of a swan's wings—and settled into sleep again.

The entire room was white: a room of snow—but warm: an igloo.

Having no senses of its own, the room could not immerse them in Anna: it could only allow her to penetrate it, closing up again round her when she was in, lodging her there in the perfect homogeneity of her style with its own. It was as though between this room and Anna there was a genetic resemblance, a line of descent: as though it was a womb: into which, a newly born cherub in her early forties, she was always welcome to creep back.

The room's receptiveness was, of course, a medallion image stamped in it by the senses of the woman who had created it, between whom and Anna, as Anna had known for a long time, the relation was that of mother to adopted daughter: the woman in her early fifties an adoptive mother to the woman in her early forties.

Anna's hostess was, in fact, the least virginal of women to have created for herself a white bedroom— least virginal, but most bridal: four times married: and only in this, her fourth married home, had she let her infatuation with white romp to the extreme of covering her whole bedroom with it—such an excess of satin purity, so blazoned, as to be not pure at all, but rioting, sensuous, shameless, like white lilac.

Presented, by her husband's wealth, with a perfectly meted-out plain little cube to play with—by a sort of inversion of a child's being given a building block to play with; the player placed inside a hollowed-out building block—this woman had set ingeniously about making it rounded: perhaps because she was a rounded little woman herself; perhaps to mark its change of status from utilitarian servant's to mistress's bedroom; perhaps in perversity, the sheer spirit of rococo. The walls' plumbness she had turned into plumpness by hanging them with some rich white material that had a pile: it did not look like anything so plain as paper, though it might in fact be paper, but as the rich understood it. The white carpet was overlaid by circular rugs, also white but of a deeper texture. The curved dressing table was quilted in white. So were the bed and its headboard. The bed, shaping itself to its mistress, was oval and perhaps for that reason ambiguous in size: was it single or double? The mystery of wealthy marriages—they always had separate bedrooms. Yet Anna would not have entered so confidently had this been her host's bedroom as well.

Sometimes, pursuing her psychological perception as a fantasy, Anna asked herself whether she could have been the child of her adoptive mother's husband —of any of them: but she seemed to carry not a trait of resemblance— to any of them: and they, as a matter of fact, seemed to have nothing in common with one another except wealth and wife. Anna in this adoptive friendship was wholly her mother's daughter.

The adoption was emphasised by her being named, accidentally, for her mother: they were both Anne. The younger had politely ceded her name and become Anna (which had suggested to her to become, for the ball, Donna Anna). She was not Anna in every company, but only for the convenience of people who knew both Annes—which included, ex officio, Anne's husband, who was neither receptive nor antagonistic towards Anna but treated her less as a person than as a foible of his wife's. Anne married exclusively men who could afford to indulge her foibles: after announcing her engagement to her fourth fortune, she had said to Anna 'My dear, you look at me cynically. I think you think of me as one who has loved not well but too wisely.' All her husbands indulged her ambition towards her purely white room, and if its achievement had been delayed till recently it must be through emotional not economic inhibitions.

Achieved under the fourth, the room had been made the setting for ornaments—Anna perhaps among them—devoutly collected under earlier régimes. The alpine whiteness was pierced by coloratura moments, flowerings of confectioner's colour, always unnatural and sometimes anti-natural in heraldic or tropical extravagance. Above the bed, half of an opened Chinese umbrella, struts solidified into brass, silk into iridescent enamel, afforded the occupant or occupants fantasy protection from fantasy weather. A gilt cartouche, German rococo, bursting at all its tips like buds of foliage, finally broke into moistureless waves over a placidly white wall. Two cherubs' heads— two cherubs' knobs—conferred tête à tête under a cornice; a flutter of wing beneath them made a conversational gesture as it might be of the hand they were whispering behind. From the mantel as from the sea emerged a porcelain pedestal, white and gold, at once seashell, mollusc's foot and exotic island, on which a Chelsea shepherd for ever gave tuition on the flute to a Chelsea shepherdess for ever unlearning of both the arts he was trying to teach; she sat without expression, a lamb in her lap and her tutor's arms about her neck; while behind the whole group an asymetrical blackthorn of inorganic green bloomed in grainy, brain-like white clumps of cauliflower.

From the room's shiny surfaces of white, the eye seemed continually slipping off, slipping down, as though your eyelids were being pulled shut and your body being depressed towards floor or bed in a delicious swoon that was half laziness. The whole room tugged, with its own gravitation, against the vertical, drooping and bending under its own heaviness as under an armful of lilacs, Anna, upright in the centre of it all, saw herself, with her head and most of her legs chopped off, in her hostess's looking glass. A middle view of her own vertically, it shewed chiefly her black dress, though it included her pale upper arms, thin as the body of a stick insect, and the bare skeleton of her shoulders and collar bone, harnessed by the dress's two broad black straps. It made, in the whiteness, a photograph of too high contrast. Only the Siamese kitten on the bed behind mediated between the tones, a small tussock the colour of snow turned slushy in the street.

Without touching or addressing the kitten, or even properly looking at it, though with an awareness of it as if it had been a temple idol not merely collected but seriously invoked by her friend up here in solitude, Anna walked past the bed and into the little bathroom, where she creamed her face out of Anne's jar of cold cream, wiped it on Anne's tissues, dashed it with water from Anne's basin, which was a modern, fake rococo shell with a single mixer tap, and dried herself in one of Anne's white towels.

She came back into the bedroom and opened her small suitcase on the bed, accidentally creating a declivity in the quilted surface into which the kitten tumbled with resentment. She spread her jars and bottles on the dressing table, pushing to one side the tiny snuff box Anne kept there for pins, and seated herself in the white, buttoned

19

tub armchair, pulling it up to the dressing table so that at last her face, and only her face, came into position in the looking glass.

Very swiftly she rubbed foundation over and into her face, with hands that were long, ineluctably competent and much too bony, like the hand of death in a gruesome marble tombscape—but with deep pink fingernails.

She sat back, waiting for the foundation to set, her lids lowered so as not to disturb the forming surface. When her skin began to prickle, she very cautiously flickered her eyes open and leaned forward to confirm in the mirror image that surface and dressing had fused without blemish, and that her face was ready for her.

She sat before her face: painter before primed canvas, potter before bisque, gilder before wood on which the gesso had been laid. She behaved without hurry or excitement and almost without thoughts, in the craftsman's near-automatism, his subjection of his mind to his skill.

To her dispassionate artificer's gaze her face gazed beadily back. In the centre of the eighteenth-century glass it pouted in the same style as the rococo frame. Pouches beneath her eyes, puffing like cherubs' profiles, seemed to continue the dressing table's quilting into the face; Anna's nose, triangular and truncated as the nose—or the hat, or the whole person—of a chinoiserie Chinaman, served only to button down the flesh for a central moment, after which it cushioned out on every side with the apple surface of wax round a seal's imprint, until it was gathered again and came puckering in to form the mouth, which drooped asymetrically, small, deep—a rosebud, but bruised.

Very carefully but still almost unthinkingly Anna chose, among her little disk-shaped boxes, so much smaller than Anne's pin box, the one which contained silver and turquoise. She wanted a metallic suggestion and at the same time a suggestion of patina, but of patina not wholly opaque and not virulent. To metal she wanted to fuse porcelain— she wanted, in fact, lustre; and this the silver ingredient was to supply: but she did not want to forfeit the translucence of porcelain, and by choosing a colour which contained blue she meant to catch the kind of bluish ceramic glaze which embodied, in a tone like the shadowed parts of milk, the blue tint of flesh above a vein.

After swivelling open the lid of the box, a disk rotating round a disk, she touched the cushion of her little finger to the cushion of eye shadow, transferred its load to her eyelid, pressed, and then raised her finger as delicately as a leaf which had discharged its quota of gold. Remembering the exact amount of pressure she had given to eye shadow and lid, she measured it out again for the other eye. In the glass she scrutinised first one closed lid and then the other. She had given them a look of such translucence that it seemed to be the green-blue colour of her own irises which was shewing through.

Anna opened a bottle of chalky grey liquid, picked out the finest of her brushes and began to inscribe a grey line along her lid above the lashes, noticing that she must be bodily relaxed since the skin accepted the brush instead of puckering before it like water before a prow. The door of the bedroom opened with a padded sound, its action muffled by the quilting inside. Anna saw, in a corner of the glass, a fold of gold lamé, and Anne said:

'My dear. You're up *here*.'

'I ran away.'

'So have I. How lovely to find you.' She kissed the top of Anna's head, a thing she could do only when Anna was sitting down.

Anna laid aside her brush and turned to look at the short plump dumpy woman undulating in gold lamé behind the chair. 'I haven't seen you all evening. I suppose one never *sees* one's hostess. How are you? Also, incidentally, who are you?'

'Don't you know the news? Queen Anne is dead.'

'Queen Anne.' Anna contemplated her.' Hence the regal gold?'

'Hence. I'm so glad if it is regal. At first I thought purple velvet. Then I thought No, not on *me*. As for white—people would think I was marrying again.'

'You're not, by the way?'

'Anna, don't try to be shocking.'

Anna laughed. It came into her mind that the essence of

her friend's resemblance to the queen, and of the queen's to her rôle, was that both perfectly resembled a solid gold orb: you could sense yourself assessing its weight in the palm of your hand.

'I've usurped your dressing table,' Anna said, making apologetically as if to rise.

Anne patted her down. 'Get on with doing your pretty face. Mine's beyond repair.'

Anna turned back to the mirror. 'Pretty face?' she said, looking at it, groping with her hand for her brush. 'The face of a discontented lapdog about to sneeze.'

'O my dear,' Anne protested, but laughing. Anna unscrewed the grooved metal stick with which she put on mascara and twisted herself sideways so that she could see in the glass the mascara's moment of contact with her lashes.

Anne sat down on the bed, making another and much greater declivity into which the kitten rolled unable to recover itself. She picked it up and held it with its cheek beside her own, presently carrying it across and standing behind Anna's chair. 'This is my discontented lapcat.'

High above Anna's shoulder the kitten stared at its own face in the glass. In a parallel gaze, Anna stared at her face. For a few seconds there was a contest of narcissisms. Then Anna yielded and transferred her gaze from her own reflexion to the kitten's. It went on staring at itself.

'How did anyone ever suppose,' Anna asked, 'that blue eyes betoken honesty and frankness?'

'Don't you like him?'

'I respect him.'

In silence they all three stared at the kitten's face.

Suddenly the kitten let out a monstrous 'Caw caw caw,' opening its mouth very wide with each noise, more like a baby bird than a cat, and not pausing to draw breath between.

Anne took it back to the bed, where it settled in her lap. 'I know,' she said, 'that you're Donna Anna. Someone told me. Of course I knew it would be something from Mozart.'

'Mm,' said Anna, her mouth distorted and gagged in the effort of precision as she made up her eyelashes.

'You've heard Rudy's joke?'

'Mm.'

Reverting, Anne said:

'Your face isn't a bit like a lapdog's. More like a cherub's.'

Anna held her eyes purposely startled and unblinking, to give the mascara time to dry. Propelling the mascara stick back into its holder, she said:

'Then perhaps I should have come as Cherubino.'

'O my dear you *should*. To shew off your lovely legs.'

'Bony,' said Anna. 'Indecent to reveal so much of one's skeleton while one yet lives.'

'You should experience being buried alive in a tomb of flesh,' said Anne. 'If you knew how I envy you your figure.'

Anna picked out a lipstick, one of the long thin ones, pulled off its cap and held it up, preparatory, in the admonishing position of John the Baptist's forefinger. 'No you don't. You know yours is much more appealing in bed.'

'My *dear*,' said Anne, despairingly. She made a sling of her two hands joined, eased it under the cat curled in her lap, and carefully, like the slowest and smoothest of cranes, raised him, swung him clear and lowered him without disturbance on to the bed. But the cat instantly jumped up, shook himself and turned completely about before settling again in exactly the position Anne had given him to begin with. 'You're as perverse as this cat. What *is* your mood tonight? Morbid? Cynical?'

Hesitating with the lipstick at her lips, Anna replied:
'I mistrust tonight.'

'Yes, new year. Hateful new years.'

With a lipstick of enamel pink Anna precisely outlined the involuted border of the left half of her upper lip. Starting at the outside right, she brought the other line to meet it. She filled in the colour, blunted it on a tissue and then, having created half an enamel rose, paused to ask:

'If you hate new years, why celebrate them?'

'It's not me, darling. It's Tom-Tom.'

Anna coloured her lower lip in one deep curve. 'Darling, does he *like* being called by that absurd name?'

'Darling, he gets furious if people *don't*.'

Anna dabbed powder over her face, covering the newly coloured lips, which she presently cleared by using the lipstick again, this time as a snow plough. On her cheeks she smoothed in the powder with a baby's hairbrush. 'There. Finished,' she said, before she was, wiping her fingers on a tissue like a priest after communion, tumbling her apparatus back into her case like a doctor or a children's entertainer after a visit, and re-instated Anne's snuff box in the centre of the dressing table. Her hand paused, went back to the snuff box and picked it up. She rose, vacating the chair, offering it back to Anne, even while she pored over the snuff box's floral top. 'Pretty thing.'

'Yes,' said Anne, rising from the bed.

'And yet, you know,' Anna said, putting the snuff box down again, 'in all eighteenth-century pottery there's that hint . . .'

'That hint?' asked Anne, sitting heavily in the vacated chair like a fat Italian taking his turn in the barber's shop.

'Of the chamber pot,' said Anna.

'*What* a mood. What a *mood*,' said Anne.

'I'm angry with myself.' It was spoken emptily, in a voice that put you in mind of the suck-back of an ebbing wave and of the chilliness after swimming.

'What have you done?'

'I told you. Run away.'

'What from?'

'O—the implications of being Donna Anna.'

'I don't,' Anne said, lying back in her chair, 'understand you. What made you come as Donna Anna, anyway?'

'O, we poor,' said Anna, walking round the bed for the sake of walking, 'we don't have *psychology,* my dear. We merely have shifts and exigencies. A black dress the poor have always with them. Ergo, one comes as a bereaved daughter.'

'You're not poor.'

'No, of course I'm not. But you *are* rich.'

'How inimical you sound tonight.'

'Dear Anne, dear Anne.' Anna let herself fall forward on to the bed, disturbing the kitten again. I'm sorry, dearest Anne. And sorry to have upset your kitten. But you know, I always have to warn myself against you.'

'Warn yourself, dear child?'

'When 'I'm here, I might almost think this was *my* room, as though I were as rich as you. No, it's not that. But there is a conflict of interest somewhere—or, if there *were* to be one—if it came to a crisis—'

'Well?' Anne's voice was steadfast.

'O, you'll expel me from your igloo some day,' Anna said. 'Aren't you going to do your face?'

'I tell you, it's beyond salvage. That's not what I came for. I'd never *mean* to expel you, you know.'

'What *did* you come for?'

Anne's plump hand, satirically furtive, tugged open one of the drawers of the dressing table, slipped in and came out clenched round half a dozen of the expensive peppermint creams she bought, in packages shaped like flower baskets, from a café in Wigmore Street.

She offered in gesture to throw one to Anna, who shook her head: Anne put the sweet in her own mouth: 'Darling,' said Anna, 'even your vices are white—and so expensive.'

As Anne sucked, the scent of mint crept into the room and hung, palpable as drapery, pungent, pervasive. The nose overwhelmingly suggested to the eye that the white-hung room must be a bower of flowering mint, like the blackthorn bower behind the Chelsea rustics.

'Minthe was a nymph,' Anna said.

'I,' said Anne, putting another sweet in her mouth, 'am anything but. Have you noticed, by the way, that both you and I have come as people of our own real name? Now what does that signify? How honest we are? That we're opposed to disguises?'

'No, the opposite. We're unwilling to reveal ourselves. We won't give away what our daydreams are.'

'People come to fancy dress balls as their daydreams?'

'Why else should the least witty man in the world come as Voltaire? The lady in London least likely to commit adultery as Lady Hamilton?'

Laughing, protesting, salivating, Anne said:

'All right, two examples, but you can't build a theory on two examples. What about Rudy?'

'Even Rudy would like to be a poet.'

28

'Well . . . Maybe.' Anne swallowed her peppermint and began another.

'I daresay bankers often would. I don't know many bankers.'

'No, wait,' Anne said, talking hastily round her new mouthful, 'I can refute you: Marie Antoinette.' She swallowed. 'There are at least five Marie Antoinettes in the house tonight.'

'All women want to have their heads chopped off,' Anna replied. 'Don't you know that yet?'

Anne let her hands, from which she had finished all the peppermints, flop over the sides of her chair. It was meant as a gesture of giving Anna up, but evidently it brought home to her how weary she was: she pushed off her shoes and extended her legs, and then, like a sculptor deciding the points of support for a figure, arranged herself with the round back of her heels propped on the floor and the round back of her head against the chair. Eyes shut, voice drowsing, she said:

'We must go back to the party. It calls me from below, like knowing something's on in the kitchen.'

'Let it seethe,' said Anna, immobile on the bed.

'No, really . . .'

'All right. Let's go.'

Neither of them moved. The only sound was the kitten's breathing which, strained through its fur, whistled thinly like the night wind in a melodrama.

'All the same, I don't believe you want your head chopped off,' Anne said, without opening her eyes, 'even though you might deserve it. But I'm blessed if I see what you do want.' Anna did not reply, so Anne elaborated: 'What do you want, I mean, as Donna Anna? I feel sure that's the clue to your mood tonight. To be seduced by Don Giovanni?'

After a moment Anna said carefully:

'I met a Don Giovanni.'

'Really? Is there one here?' Anne opened her eyes, as though he could be in her bedroom, 'I haven't seen half the guests. Another reason why I must get back to the party. I probably don't *know* half the guests. Such a lot of them are Tom-Tom's friends . . .' And then, having talked her thoughts to the point: 'Was it Don Giovanni you ran away from? From your fate?'

'But what *is* Donna Anna's fate?' Anna lazily asked.

'Well, to be seduced by Don Giovanni.'

'But *is* she?' Anna insisted—but faintly.

'Well, my dear, Act One Scene One—I mean, the woman comes tumbling out of her house in the middle of the night trying to stop him getting away before she can unmask him and yelling blue murder or, rather, blue rape. . .'

'Yes, but has he succeeded,' Anna asked, not permitting her voice or body to betray any interest in the outcome, 'or has he only tried?'

'Well, I'd always assumed—' Anne stopped short. 'Of course she *says* it was only an attempt. But she'd *have* to say that, wouldn't she? I mean, it *was* the eighteenth century, and there was her honour, and that wet fiancé of hers to be considered. And the poor thing *was* Spanish . . .'

'Even so,' said Anna. 'It doesn't absolutely preclude that she was telling the truth.'

'I think the audience is meant to assume . . .'

'How can the audience judge? Whatever happens happens before the curtain goes up.'

'You could hardly expect it to happen on stage,' said Anne.

'That's assuming it *does* happen,' said Anna.

They both laughed, and both fell silent.

'Perhaps,' said Anne presently, whispering under the enchantment of the idea, 'if one listened very attentively to the music of the overture it would turn out to be describing what's taking place just before the curtain goes up.'

'Ah, if only one could—in that sense—*read* music.' Anna suddenly jumped to her feet, startling the kitten. 'Come on, Anne. Come back to your party.'

'Coming'—not coming, still lying in the chair.

'No, really.'

Anne began to rise, grunting into her shoes.

'You're throwing a ball,' Anna said. 'It's too good to throw away.'

'What a sweet thing to say,' Anne said, following Anna to the door. 'May I tell Tom-Tom you said it?'

'Seriously, darling,' Anna asked again, as she opened the door, '*does* he like being called that?'

'My dear, I tell you . . .' Anne decided to shut the door again. She drew Anna back secretively into the white bosom of the room. 'Listen, dearest. Do you believe there are intimacies of married life one ought not to reveal even to one's best friend?'

'No; certainly not when you're obviously proposing to reveal one.'

'Well, listen.' Anne confronted her. 'He's Tom-Tom.' Her face searched, almost anxiously, up into Anna's. 'I'm Tum-Tum.'

Anna gaped in horror down at her friend before starting to giggle. Anne started to giggle, too. Both giggling, they fumbled the light off and got the door opened and themselves into the corridor, where they stepped into the feeble shuffling noise of party talk and dancing in the distance below, with a thin treble intimation of the band. Anne closed the door of her bedroom behind them and as she did so Anna, though still giggling, thought with sharp, sensuously experienced sadness that the smell of mint which was now being shut into the room in the dark would soon shrivel and vanish, like a corpse entombed, like fruits in a garden whose owner had gone away after locking the gate.

3

Coming down the grand staircase by Anne's stately side, Anna distinguished, in the crowd below, the quaint fat man who, when you looked down on him from above, as Anna seemed always to do, resembled a boiled egg. He still seemed alone—more than ever so, since he was now without even his cup of coffee. Yet he still had the air of protecting something: his opalescent waistcoat, perhaps, or his paunch, or his sense of being himself.

For the space of a couple of descending steps Anna let her eye pursue his meanderings through the crowd. Rather, that turned out to be a railway station illusion, and it was the crowd which was sifting past him, while he stood stock—protectively—still

Fluttering with the little streamers of crowd past him, Anna's gaze was drawn to distinguish someone else—or, at least, something else: a flash of black costume. She did not allow it to imprint more than an impressionistic wisp across her vision but withdrew her gaze and—in so suddenly shortening its reins— half-stumbled on a chair.

She clutched for Anne's arm but did not need to make contact with it before recovering herself.

Even so, she had already said, quickly, like an excuse or a minor curse on being clumsy:

'I should have come as Cherubino after all. It would have been easier than a skirt for the stairs.'

Anne, pursuing her own thickly flowing course— a golden syrup of lamé—and intent on controlling the heavy resistances of her own skirt, as though intent on wading, replied without haste and without looking at Anna:

'On second thoughts, darling, you *are* a little old to play Cherubino.'

Anna laughed, made on an indrawn breath a sound — 'O, O'—as though to indicate a touch at fencing, and looked ahead to the foot of the staircase where the hostess's approach had been observed. Two or three guests seemed to be leaping up towards her already; and the impression that these were Anne's dogs, over-excited by the thought that she was going to exercise them, was lent detail by the three rows of precisely crimped curls which ran along the sides of some of the men's wigs and which could be read as the horizontal bars of waves shimmying down a cocker spaniel's ears.

Descending deeper, nearer them, further into the party roar, Anna's mind re-interpreted the silken waves into ocean waves, which crashed against the staircase, casting up a sprinkling of foam and laughter, making fingers which encroached graspingly, but as lazily as caterpillars, up on to the second, on to the third, step. Round the terminal of the outward-curling banisters one young man had arched himself backwards, catwise, like a wave slicing itself on a breakwater, and from this unexpected direction his arm pussyfooted higher than anyone else's, an inlet of foam making towards Anne's descending ankles.

Yet though it seemed as much to be taken seriously as a brute, inanimate element, this was still a personal sea, not merely encroaching but predatory and selective, the sea in a Greek myth, reaching up to snatch Anne and leave Anna alone.

Anne, however, descending into it as imperturbably as if she was going to bathe, and paying Anna the compliment of not directing her attention to it one moment before its touch should actually claim her flesh, went on:

'So, my dear'— this was the first time Anna realised that her friend's thought had not been completed—'you have no choice but to be Donna Anna. The question is only what you're going to do.'

'Do?' Anna said gaily, at the very moment that her foot, in guardsman's harmony with her friend's, touched the floor. 'Throw myself into your ball, of course.'

Importunities plucked at Anne, the polite over-eagerness of guests. But Anne, as though she had so far only paddled into the verge of the sea and crossed only the technical border between land and ocean, waded—stumped—on, the importunate guests going with her, as it were backwards, higgledy-piggledy, head-over-heels: if they seemed to cling to her, she seemed to lift them clean off their feet, to be actually carrying them, she a champion, they mere nothings. Yet as she went in deeper, encountering thicker crowd, the nothings, too, so easy to lift up once, seemed to make their weight felt with being carried a distance. Anne's stumpings became more widely spaced; her footsteps, more weightily planted, began to shiver with each impact of planting and to heave, quake, almost refuse, at each effort at transplanting.

Anna, meanwhile, trying to follow a parallel course, was buffeted by the eddies thrown off round Anne's progress. Shoulders wheeled into her, knocked her aside and made her lose way; and so Anne had to turn not merely to the side but completely round in order to make sure that Anna was still present and within earshot when she asked:

'No—I mean do about the Don?'

'O my dear—' Anna began to throw her reply despairingly, a lifeline that would never reach its destination across the storm. Before she could finish, Anne had crossed the border which took her out of her depth. Anna lost sight of her.

When she recovered it, she perceived that Anne had at last surrendered to the exchange and had suffered the nothings she had been carrying to carry her. The border they had lifted her across was the double doorway into the ballroom. She was already on the dance floor. One of the nothings had importuned successfully. Even in his arms, however, she was looking back, round his shoulder, towards the edge, towards Anna; and Anna, dodging this way and that like a spectator at a procession, was trying to make her face visible to Anne so that her answer could be lipread if not heard.

Already Anne was launched on the waves of dancers. Anna saw her breasting the rhythm of the music, buoyant in her obesity. She plunged, nodded, seemed about to sink, and swam—a great rippling, obese, sleek golden seal. Anna felt it was to a departing merman that she called and mouthed:

'I'm too old for adventures. Too old.'

'Too *what*, Anna?' said Rudy Blumenbaum's voice: his unmistakable voice: a dark baritone which every now and then rose into a squeak, as though Rudy was deeply snoring and yet whistling at the same time: and as the tone rose to falsetto, so Rudy's accent become tinged with cockney.

Anna turned and held out both hands to him. 'Too old, Rudy.'

He squeezed her hands. 'Now listen, dearie. You've heard you're as *old* as you feel? Well, you'—he converted his hand-squeezing into slipping his arm round her waist and squeezing that—'feel pretty good to me. Care to dance?'

His grip transformed itself again, now into a dancer's grip, and before she had time to assent he had her with her back to the dance floor ready to begin.

'Rudy,' she said, protesting at his swiftness, 'I don't know that I still *can*.'

She meant she was still aching from the Scottish dancing, but he took it for another allusion to her age: he broke off, reached round behind her and gave her a little slap on the bottom. 'Get along with you,' he said, resuming her hand like reins and giving her toes a neat little kick with his own. He danced her out into the middle of the floor, making her feel like a mare being given its first outing of the day by a jaunty head lad. Rudy *was* a rather horsey—a lightweight, an almost bow-legged—little man.

4

Crouched between the wall and the inmost pier glass in the ladies' cloakroom, Ruth Blumenbaum opened her notebook, turned back to the beginning and read through the entry she had already made.

This notebook seems almost too nice to spoil.
I love new stationery.
12.10 p.m. Meant to get away to start diary long before this but held up.

Ruth interrupted her reading and, using her white silk-covered knees as a desk, scribbled out *p.m.* and wrote in *a.m.*

Anyway, got to house about 10.20. Daddy had trouble parking on slight hill. V. sophistd. hour to start party, but b/se of new year's eve, of course. All the way in the car Mummy kept saying we cd. leave any time after midnight, but sure D. will not want to. As soon as we arrived had to sep. from Daddy to leave coats. 'Run and park your coats, ladies,' D. said, 'hope Anne has not had parking meters

installed up there.' Actually she has had a lot of mirrors
installed—and her housekeeper (I think: familiar, anyway).
Tickets for coats, wh. are put on long trestle table—like
bazaar. Mummy's fur much nicest of those piled on table
but wish she (M.) had made some effort at 18th c. costume.
When saw housekeeper in cloakroom was afraid wd. not be
able to creep away here to write up diary—wd. not want
to be questioned by hskpr. But fortunately when came here
to write it (12. 10) hskpr. not here. (Rather bad: anyone
cd. steal coats.) Ought to have explained at start that want
to keep diary on spot of first ball ('a great event in a girl's
life'—Mummy) to have exact record of how felt at time:
b/se am sure most people falsify when they remember such
things afterwards. Am sure Mummy was not like she says
she was when young. D. doesn't talk much about his youth.
Cd. have saved time by explaining purpose of diary at home
before leaving. But want it all done on spot. Won't alter
after, either. Then notebook can become RELIC *like Elisabeth*
B. was always talking about.

Next to the name Elisabeth B., Ruth wrote in an aster-
isk and annotated it—sideways up the margin: *Cath. girl*
at schl.

Anyway after fuss to get D. and M. to let me come didn't feel
partic, excited. Left cloakroom with M. and almost at once
met Edward. He was silly and aggressive about my costume—

said he didn't like it. I expect he didn't understand when
I told him who I was. He is v. badly educated: anyway,
about cultured things. I thought he was trying to spoil my
confidence at start of evening. He was all in black, says he
is Casanova, wh. is silly at his age.Wish men were not all so
aggressive or at least wish I was not depressed by it. Note:
They can't all be. D. is a man.Went down to ballroom and
danced twist, 2 tangoes, 1 slow fox with Ed. and 1 slow waltz
with Rex (man Ed. knows: v. tall: Cambridge) wh. made Ed.
jealous, I think. Had sandwiches (turkey and pâté) with Ed.
Drank gin and French. Quite interestg. conversn., which is
why did not get away to write diary. Ed. says he is a realist.
Saw Anna K. was here. Then Scottish dancing began, wh. I
hate, but went through with it to prove to Ed. I was not
affected, wh. he had just said I was during conversn, over
sandwchs. Saw D. was dancing (he is in Scotch costume, of
course, appropriate to Scotch dancing) and also Mummy!! D.
v. gay. He is so funny at parties, just as he is at home, not shy
at all—most people like him, even Ed. People v. much amused
by his joke about who he is. Saw Anna K. was dancing in
D.'s set If I have to speak to her wonder if I ought to call her
Anna or Mrs. K. She will call me Ruth of course, but that is
b/se she has known me since I was a child. She prob. won't
recognise me anyway. At midnight band played Auld Lang
Syne. Afterwards people kissed. Ed. suddenly took a whistle
out of his pocket and blew it. Hideous noise. Saw D. had
ended up next to Anna K. and wondered if he wd. kiss her but

of course he kissed M. instead. Ed. kissed me. Not a success.
Like when he kissed me at Xmas, really. Feel v. depressed, not
just by Ed. but by all the people, men and women, kissing.
Anna K. kissed a man in a black mask. Feel there is something
awful about all the people in the world, can't think what
they are here for— they don't seem to matter—they are like
atoms— they just move around without aim attracted or
repelled by each other; hardly matters which. Anna K. is the
most attractive woman I have ever seen. I detest her.

At the bottom Ruth wrote:
None of this expresses what I feel at all
before beginning her next entry:
   1.25 a.m.

'Rudy, you *can't* have a daughter old enough to come to
a ball.'

'No use saying I can't, Anna. My accountant assures me I
have. You should see what her fancy dress cost me.'

'But Rudy. Last time I saw her she was—what? Twelve?'
Anna jerked her cheek away from its impersonal proximity to Rudy's in order to look at his face. She was startled,
as she always was when she saw it close to, by the high
contrast of his colouring: he had a heavy blue stubble, but
the rest of his skin was a bright, transparent, easily per-
spiring crimson, the skin of a youth not old enough to
grow a beard, so that his face, as well as his voice, seemed

a physiological impossibility. 'Her name's Ruth, isn't it? Have I remembered right?'

'Mm-hm.'

'O well. I expect last time I saw her I said you *couldn't* have a daughter of twelve.'

'And I expect I said what a lot it was costing to educate her.'

They laughed. Anna's cheek returned to its slot above Rudy's shoulder, parallel with Rudy's cheek; not touching his, but receptive of the warmth issuing from it as palpably as from the radiator grille of an electric fire.

'Fortunately,' Anna said, 'you're made of money. Aren't you, Rudy?'

'Yes,' he said, 'and you're made of flesh and blood, but you'd squeal if you had to part with any, just the same.'

Anna laughed and danced on, anaesthetised to effort; it seemed that Rudy, his face invisible to her, had become a machine and that he was supplying the motive power as well as steering. Her eyes, invisible to his, felt free to sweep the ballroom: dancing had none of the intimacy of conversation face to face: her vision swept and swooped, taking in whatever Rudy put it in her way to see—but he himself, of course, was not seeing what she saw; he was merely the machine, or the operator hidden beneath the rather jerky, bumpy motor which impelled the switchback car on its route, from which she observed, as chance allowed, swathes of landscape, each suddenly cut off and replaced by another.

She was not startled even when she glimpsed the black costume and black mask, lurking—like one of Francesco Guardi's impressionistic cloaked figures in the colonnade of the Doges' Palace—among the spectators at the edge of the ballroom. She felt as safe as a passenger on a switch-back in a thriller, whose enemy had been left in the fairground below. She did not mind if Don Giovanni saw her, since Rudy's arms must proclaim her safe: Rudy's very arms must proclaim that Rudy was monogamous and devoted to his wife and daughter: and in any case Rudy's arms quickly swept her round and presented the other side of the ballroom to her view, so that Don Giovanni, if he did see her, must do so without her knowing whether he had or not and without, therefore, establishing communication or even communion of minds.

'. . . the absolute earth', Rudy was saying, 'to educate her. And the object of the whole exercise was to convince her her father is vulgar.'

'O Rudy,' Anna began: but something warm and like the slap of a wave caressed itself against her back, and Anne's voice whispered:

'How's the Don?'

'Don't know. Don't care. I'm on the run,' Anna replied, twisting round, searching over her shoulder for the woman who had been behind her. But the whirligig of the dance had reversed them. It was Anne's partner who presented himself to Anna's vision; and it turned out that Anne was now dancing with her great shambling, shapeless husband, behind whom even she was obliterated from sight.

'Tom-Tom—hullo.'

'Anna—goodbye.'

'Tom-Tom's in great form tonight,' said Rudy.

'Isn't he? So are you, Rudy.'

'You take the words out of my mouth. I've been meaning to tell you all evening. You look blooming, Anna. Really blooming.'

She thanked him. They danced. Presently, she reverted:

'Rudy, I'm sure Ruth—'

'*Won't* think me vulgar?'

'I'm sure she has enough native wit to stand out against any such idea. She must have. She's your child.'

'Ah, don't say blood is thicker than an expensive education.'

'I'm sure it is.'

'That means I've wasted my money,' said Rudy.

D. danced with Anna K. Cd. see from way she laughed at his conversatn. she sees how amusing he is. Also he is much more lively dancer than anyone else on floor, Anna K. looks rather a beanpole dancing with him, though she is not really tall. He is a bit short, of course. She is obviously charmed by him. Most people are, I suppose he finds her attractive. But can't be sure of this. Often when you think somebody so attractive everyone must notice it, people turn out never to

have given it a thought. Everyone thought Jane T. the most
beautiful girl in the school but Mummy didn't even notice
which one she was in the play. D.'s style of dancing may be
old-fashioned but it is good style. Much better that Ed.'s, Ed.
v. aggressive, so came up here to write up diary. Feel much
older than Ed. Emotionally, I mean.

'Technically, she isn't old enough to be here. Her mother
kept saying she oughtn't to go to a ball until she's come
out officially. But I said: "Go on, Mum. Even if she hasn't
come out, let her *trickle* out."'

When was a schoolgirl if I met an attractive woman I used
to fall in love w. her. Suppose this was way of not being
depressed at her being more attractive than me. (Query:
this diary too introspective? Morbid, as Ed. wd. say. Beastly
egotistical, anyway.) Used to think must be Lesbian. Looked
up Sappho and Lesbos in encycl. Liked idea of Gk. island:
sun: blue sky: playing ball on sands beside blue sea—like
one of those classical Picassos Miss L. so keen on. But do
not really care for pink, monumental women—a bit like
M.!—but cannot imagine M. playing ball w. nothing on
!! Used to wonder if when was grown-up D. wd. BUY Lesbos
for me. But all that ages ago. Realise now it was naive
idea. Mean Sappho etc. ages ago, mod. civilisn. much more
complic.d, etc. (Expect you can't buy Gk island, at least not
big one, any more, even if D. cd. and wd. Expect he cd.) But

46

way I have written it is ambiguous, cd. mean it's ages ago
that I used to think it wd. be nice—and actually this is true,
too. Cannot feel like that any more. No doubt more healthy
and normal but makes v. vulnerable to depressn. Certainly
cannot imagine loving Anna K. But people must have
done—men, I mean. She looks as if she has had lots of lovers.
Suppose I think her attractive b/se she is not monumental
type. This may mean D. does not find her attractive, as he
evidently likes monumental type, e.g. Mummy. Anna K.
more on scraggy side, like me. Actually she is not quite tall
enough. Think I am about ideal height for a woman. (Not
conceit—have many disadvantages.) Of course people of
my generation usually are taller than people of Anna K.'s—
better feeding when babies.

Anna felt a brake applied and the machinery jerk before
she realised what had prompted it to do so: a man's knuckles knocking on Rudy's back.

Rudy swung round, opening up for Anna a view of the
intruder. But she had already seen his black costume.

She felt quite palpably between her own shoulder blades
the rhythm of his knocking on Rudy's back.

She was stricken first by the panic, and then rapidly
by the embarrassment of suffering an arrest. In sheer
shyness she looked down and away. It was some seconds
before she let it seep into her vision that he was not Don
Giovanni: he was without a mask, a good deal taller than

Don Giovanni, fairer and much younger—much, much younger than either Don Giovanni or herself.

Anna and Rudy began to speak apologetically, regretfully, to one another. But the stranger ducked under the trailing grip Rudy had kept on Anna's hand, assumed her and danced her away. 'Is this an excuse me dance?' Anna asked him at once, worried.

'No. It's just that my partner's run away from me and I've got the cheek of the devil.'

'Have you?' Without attending, she submitted to the convention whereby women on a dance floor, like horses in a riding stables, must passively accept whatever partner proposed himself. It was probably because she had experienced on his behalf a panic which had turned out unneeded that she felt empty of any capacity to feel interested in him.

She was prepared for her face to fit itself into the old slot in relation to the new partner, as though the partner's personality was nothing and the only adjustment that need be made was an alteration of, as it were, stirrup length from Rudy's shortness to the young man's height. But the young man, disdaining the false intimacy of pressing his cheek against hers, thrust her away from him, trying to impose on her the true intimacy of looking him in the face, while he held her very loosely and danced in a gangling but quite practised way. She struggled for a minute against his manner of dancing: but the convention had given it to him, not her, to dictate.

'Who're you looking for?' he said.

'Looking for? No one.'

'Your eyes keep looking round the room.'

'Do they? . . . Actually, I'm avoiding someone.'

'It's the same thing, isn't it?'

'Is it?' For the first time Anna-felt an interest. She looked at him deliberately. His face, though it was pleasant, and perhaps even quite handsome, reminded her of Donald Duck's. Not that the nose was very long, but it stuck out at a sharpish angle and was flatly triangular, formed into two deep grooves like the grooves on a bill. Beneath it the mouth and chin were pushed up rather close and small-scale, like the mouth and chin beneath a cat's muzzle. The mouth was quite wide across the face but thin- and smooth-lipped, the chin quite sharply defined but delicate: a little pussy's mouth and chin, and not really any more gentle. His colouring was pink and gold. He probably had little incisive white teeth, like a pussy. His small, bright-eyed face turned brightly this way and that, as though he moved it by pulling a rod and was deliberately giving the effect of brightness, above a tall, thin neck which perhaps had contributed to the initial thought of Donald Duck, since it had a poultry scragginess. Anna took a moment to let herself realise that his neck was thin because he was still so young: the last of the changes begun by puberty had not yet been quite completed.

'Well, you can't avoid someone if you don't know where they are.'

'O. No. I see what you mean.'

Evidently he was aware that she had lost interest; and it was presumably in a bid to bully it back that he let go of her altogether—apart from their linked hands—and left her to dance on her own while he pranced about, reminding her now of a rocking horse, no longer in front of her but beside her, letting his own gaze, this time, survey the ballroom.

Anna danced, her hand dangling by her side. Something touched her hand. She looked, saw gold lamé and then Anne, who had already danced—in orthodox fashion— past, leaving a little folded piece of paper in Anna's hand. It lay loosely, rolling as the hand dangled.

The young man swooped in on Anna, faced her again and held her again at his long arms' length in his loose embrace.

'If you danced in the old-fashioned orthodox way,' Anna said, 'my face would be up against your shoulder—like a baby being burped.'

'Yup,' he said, 'and I wouldn't be able to see your expression.'

'Neither would you be able to see me unfold and read the note which has just been put into my hand.'

'You'll have to read it under my nose. If it's a guilty secret I shall know from your face.'

'I'll have to chance it,' Anna said. She removed her hand from his shoulder and undid the note. 'With your permission.'

The handwriting was—she had feared it would not be—Anne's.

'My dear, just to convince *you there's only one rôle left to you. Rudy Blumenbaum's daughter is here as Cherubino.'*

'Good news?' said the young man. 'Football pools? Rich aunt died?'

'I don't see why I shouldn't tell you. It's hardly gossip. It says Rudy Blumenbaum's daughter is here as Cherubino.'

'I could have told you that.'

'*Could* you?'

'What I can't tell you is who on earth Cherubino is.'

'Then you know the Blumenbaums?'

'You don't think I'd cut in on a man I didn't know? He might get angry.'

'But I thought you had the cheek of the devil.'

'It's all a front,' he said. 'Like coming as Casanova.'

'O, that's who you are.'

'That's who I am. You can't get anywhere without a front, these days.'

'And you *are* getting somewhere?' Anne asked.

'My God I hope I'm getting to be Rudy Blumenbaum's son-in-law. He's *terribly* rich. Did you know that?'

'Yes.'

'Sometimes I almost faint with excitement when I think of it.'

*Don't think Ed. has ever been in love. This prob. why he
seems naive to me. Also this is source of friction, why don't
always get on. He seems to have no past, only future. At
least, only thinks of future. Mummy talks about her youth
like this— 'Everything was so fresh, you didn't know what
life was going to offer.' Think this must be falsified Anyway
what life did offer her was pretty gd.—Daddy. I don't feel
everything fresh, everything just beginning, feel a lot of
things ended for ever. As if had been brought up on island
wh. now forbidden to go back to. Or not forbidden—unable.
Island sunk, as it were. Perhaps real trouble between Ed. and
me is am already too old to love.*

'So every half hour she creeps away to fill in this diary.'

'Admirable,' Anna said, 'if a little cold-blooded.'

'Cold-blooded? I think it's sentimental. Like keeping
wax fruits under a glass dome.'

'More like keeping one's appendix in a bottle.'

'No, it's sentimental. She wants to moon over the thing
afterwards.'

'Are you sure it isn't to *prevent* her mooning afterwards?'

'Well, she certainly won't be able to do much mooning
if she's written down what I said about her costume.'

'What did you say?'

'I said I didn't want to be seen dancing with a stablehand.
Who *is* this Cherubino anyway?'

'A page.'

'You'd think she could look feminine for one evening, wouldn't you?'

'Does it offend you that she's not a sentimentalist?'

'Me? No. 'I'm a realist.'

'In what way?'

'I want money. You're nowhere without money these days.'

'What would you buy with it, if you had it?'

'Anything that took my fancy, I suppose. You haven't got money, have you?'

'No.'

'I thought not. You're not even titled?'

'No.'

'Pity. I'd have to desert you. I mean I'd have to desert you afterwards, if I made you my mistress.'

'O. Well, I daresay you would—if you did.'

'What're you thinking? That I'm cynical? That I have got the cheek of the devil after all? Or that I'd run away if you called my bluff?'

'None of them,' said Anna. 'To be frank, you don't entice me.'

'You think I'm too young for you?'

'No. Too puritanical for me.'

'Puritanical?'

'Not to have thought what you'd do with the money.'

'My God,' he said.

They danced in silence for a little.

'My God,' he repeated. 'You really are cynical. I shall warn people against you.'

Anna laughed. They danced along the edge of the ball-room.

'You steered me here,' he said. 'You're looking for that person again, the one you're avoiding.'

'Perhaps 'I'm looking to see if your partner's come back.'

'Not likely. You'd be afraid I'd desert you.'

'Actually, I was vaguely looking', Anna said, 'for a man shaped like a boiled egg. At least, he is from above. I've only seen him from above. I don't know who he is.'

'Perhaps he's only visible from above. Perhaps he disappears on ground level.'

'Perhaps.'

'Some people have personalities like that.' He stopped dancing. They were beneath the minstrels' gallery. He pointed up at its floor. 'Let's go up there and see if we can see him from above.'

'No,' said Anna.

Something small but quite heavy plopped on the floor beside her. She moved further out into the ballroom, where one or two dancers bumped her, and looked up at the gallery. Anne was up there, leaning over the parapet, grinning. Foreshortened, and apparently flattened also sideways, her face looked plumper than ever, a great loaf of raw pastry in horizontal folds, the face of a mischievous, even a half-malevolent putto seen in a distorting glass, an earth genius, a clay genius.

Another object dropped beside Anna. The next one she caught. It was a peppermint cream. She bit off half of it and then called up to the gallery:

'Delightful, but what is this? A snowstorm? A miraculous communion?'

'Confetti,' Anne replied, and disappeared.

Went back to ballroom, saw Ed. at edge of floor with Anna K. who was FEEDING *him. Don't know what, sweet / sandwich, but she bit off half and later put other half in his mouth. Felt had seen something disgusting as if it was her tongue. Or something sacrilegious: blasphemous communion or something. Admit am jealous of Anna K. Admit, admit but still feel it. It's like being told you are going to die. Can't imagine what it wd. be like to know you are dying. Can't imagine what it wd. be like to be jealous. But* AM *jealous. And of course am going to die. Everyone is. Anna K. is. When went into ballroom felt as if had been shot through heart. But am still conscious. This sounds melodramatic but is not exaggerated. This is the true account. Wonder if D. will take me home at once.*

'Anne!'

Anne fled from Anna, along the upstairs corridor, past the room which had been made over as a ladies' cloakroom, pretending not to hear Anna's pursuit. But Anna could tell, from a particular bent intentness in her friend's back and from the unaccustomed speediness of the waddle, that Anne *had* heard. She even believed she could tell, from the particularly intense undulations in the plump flesh folded round the back, that what Anne was bending over and hugging was a giggle.

Anna hurried, swerving round single promenaders and, when she met a whole clump, putting out her hand as a buffer and then using it to hold the clump stationary while she dodged round it. Her thoughts were occupied by her immediately past actions, as though at the time she had gulped them too quickly. Pushing the other half of the peppermint into her partner's mouth; leaving him without ceremony; running—tripping on her hem—up the grand staircase and from the top catching sight of Anne on her way from the minstrels' gallery; knowing from the acceleration in the quarry's steps that the quarry knew itself sighted: the sequence had printed itself, vivid as an image on the eye, in the very nerves whereby Anna's limbs recognised where they were and what they were doing. She had performed these actions without premeditation; but premeditation was determined to take place and would settle, if it had to, for taking place after the event. 'Anne!' Occupied with the past, Anna did not immediately act on a perception of the future. While Anne fled from her down the corridor, a man in black—distinctly glimpsed for a second, between promenaders, and recognised—advanced up the corridor towards Anna. Yet Anna permitted herself to go on running after Anne, on whom she was gaining: as though what she really wanted was not to overtake Anne at all but—head on, and as quickly as she could—to meet him.

She stopped just short of where he must, by now, have reached; turned; ran back up the corridor again faster than she had come and dodged into the ladies' cloakroom, where she slammed the door behind her.

She saw nothing but the two rows of pier glasses, reflecting each other.

A figure stood up, behind the furthest pier glass on the left-hand side. In Anna's eyes it represented a whole series of infractions of nature, so complex as to seem a fantasy and yet so logical in its complexity as to trap her. The person on whom she had shut the door behind her now stood before her. He had, by changing his sex, introduced himself into the ladies' cloakroom, and yet he retained the masculine costume. That costume, which had been all black, was now all white: white from top to toe: white as Anne's bedroom. 'O—*Ruth*,' Anna said. 'You frightened me.'

'Hullo Anna.'

She was a tall, bony but large-limbed girl, without resemblance to either of her parents except for a smudge of Rudy's high colour in her cheeks. She had bold features and very black hair. She was perhaps going to be beautiful.

In the white satin knee breeches her long legs were elongated almost past belief. One hand clasped a notebook as though it had been a prayer book. The other hand (Anna reconstructed that she must have been crouching down) was tugging the breeches into a more comfortable sit. The gesture of the chapel and the gesture of the stables: between them they gave her the cachet of an expensive schooling.

'I hear you're Cherubino.'

'Mm.'

'Then we're both from Mozart. I'm Donna Anna.'

'I don't know who that is.'

'From Don *Giovanni*.'

'I wouldn't know.'

'O, you should hear it. You'd like it, if you like *Figaro*.'

'I don't particularly,' said Ruth. 'We just went to it, in a school party.'

'O.'

'D'you want the loo?' Ruth gestured with her head. 'It's through there.'

'No. I just came for a moment's respite.'

'I came to write up my diary.'

Anna made a sound of assent only, not knowing whether it would hurt Ruth's feelings to discover she knew already.

'I'm keeping a diary of the ball.'

'Then you've *got* the evening,' Anna said, looking down at Ruth's notebook, 'in there, pressed like a flower.'

'I suppose so.' Ruth added, curtly: 'You're in it.'

'Am I? It gives one a curious feeling. . .'

'Only a passing reference, of course.'

'Yes, of course.'

'Well, I've finished now, anyway,' said Ruth. She pushed past Anna and left.

Anna looked into one of the pier glasses, not examining what she saw but supposing that if something was badly amiss with her make-up or costume she would notice.

She heard the door open. Anne came in.

'What're you doing up here?' Anne said. 'Why aren't you down in the thick of it with your beau?'

'He's not my beau.'

'Darling, you're not still resisting fate? You haven't run away again?'

'Anne! Listen! He's not Don Giovanni.'

'He's not?'

'I *knew* you'd misunderstood. Do you think I'm a cradle snatcher? Actually, he's Ruth Blumenbaum's beau. I came after you to explain. If you'd only waited . . .'

'Wait for *me* a second. I must go to the john.'

Anna waited.

Anne came out, tried to straighten her lamé skirt in front of one of the glasses and then put her arm through Anna's. 'Now, my dear.'

'You weren't so far out. That one is Casanova.'

'O my dear. From the sublime to the ridiculous. What a

faux pas. Well, we must start again.' Her arm still through Anna's, she led Anna out into the corridor.

'Start what again?'

'It's like having the sort of daughter who refuses to leave home. I throw you out, and you bounce back.'

'I warned you I was on the run. I kept seeing him. At least I thought I kept seeing him.'

The corridor was full of neutral figures, several of them in black, all of them incapable of engaging Anna's attention.

'Perhaps I really was looking for him,' said Anna.

'I shall lead you down the staircase again,' said Anne, 'and launch you again. You see, I'm determined.'

Arm in arm they descended the grand staircase, wheeling like a cavalry formation past the big Cupid at the turn of the stair. Perhaps because they were arm in arm or perhaps because Anne looked what she had said she was, determined, people made way for them. At the bottom, Anna said:

'Do you think one *can* be grown-up, when one has such extreme changes of mood?'

'But of course one isn't grown-up. I'm old enough to know that's an illusion.'

'My emotions go veering about as though I was Ruth Blumenbaum's age.'

'What one learns as one grows older,' said Anne, 'is that to think of oneself as Ruth Blumenbaum's age is pitching it far too high. We're much younger than that, you and I. We're mere tots.'

'You even *look* like a tot,' said Anna, looking at her. 'It's your tendency to toddle.'

'Obscene word,' said Anne, pulling a face. 'In English it's always the apparently innocent words that sound obscene . . . Listen, my dear.' She unlinked her arm from Anna's. 'Come or not, as you please, but I must go and talk to some of my obscene guests.'

She moved into the crowd. Anna went swiftly after her, catching her round the upper arm. 'Anne,' she whispered into Anne's ear.

'My dear?'

'Anne, find him for me, please. Please find him.'

5

Without logical support, Anna felt confident that Anne would be able to find him: because he was her guest. Anne seemed to abet her in the opinion. She questioned Anna with the calming confidence of a policeman undertaking to find a lost child's mother.

'Well, medium height,' Anna replied. 'Medium age. Black costume. And a black mask.'

'Eye mask?'

'More than that. Covering all the upper part of the face. A domino. At least, I think that's what a domino is.'

'And you're sure he's not dancing?'

'Pretty sure.'

'Let's try in here, then. Is he here?'

'No.'

Anne shut the door she had opened. 'You didn't have a hallucination, did you?'

'No.'

'Sure?'

'He probably has an objective existence,' Anna said, 'in Ruth Blumenbaum's diary. She's keeping a diary of the ball.'

Anne ignored that, because she had had another thought:

'My dear. Suppose he's taken off the mask?'

'O, if he's taken *off* the mask,' Anna said, as if giving up, 'I probably wouldn't recognise him.'

'Well, well,' Anne said reassuringly, 'he must realise that himself, so he probably *won't* take it off.'

'I'd recognise him if he kissed me.'

'Dearest child, I really can't ask each of my guests to kiss you.'

'Even I', said Anna, 'wouldn't really want you to.'

Someone, passing, called to Anne:

'Lovely party, Anne.'

'All the lovelier for having you in it,' Anne called back, without in the least interrupting her conversation with Anna. 'Have you looked in the supper room?'

'No.'

'Well, let's try in there.' As they went: 'Didn't it occur to you the poor man might be hungry? Are you heartless?'

'I don't think he eats much. Now I come to remember, he's rather lean.'

'O my dear, it's always the lean ones that eat. The fat ones'—Anne smoothed her hands over her lamé hips—'are the ones that *nibble*. Well?' She had thrown open the door. 'Is he eating?'

A trestle table ran the length of the room: over it, a white linen table cloth; on it, precious, hideous silver

63

vessels. Anna was put in mind first of altars, then of wedding receptions—specifically Anne's wedding receptions; a collective memory: such a length of white table cloth could only have been hired. Behind the table stood a manservant whom Anne had not merely hired but fitted out with some eighteenth-century-suggesting clothes—in reality, Anna supposed, someone's or some club's livery. Behind *him*, in the niche of the shuttered window, stood a vast pottery urn, a funerary urn, full of irises and daffodils. The flowers looked hired, too: by which Anna meant that Anne had obviously not arranged them herself but had had them done by the florist.

A few guests stood about the room, eating. A few dishes of food stood about the table, partly eaten. Where there had been piles of sandwiches there were now sheer, unsteady towers, a single sandwich wide —the section with the flag or the cress on top, which no one had liked to take. Upside down, polished, a mass of clean wine glasses was marshalled at one end of the table. The rest of the table was littered with used glasses, some standing actually in the dishes, some propped, the dregs of liquid tilted in the bottom of the glass, already turning sticky and beginning to crystallise. Lying in one silver dish, not quite in contact with the untouched sandwiches, was a sandwich half eaten. The edges of the bread were beginning to curl apart; a death's head grinning. The granules of the surface of the white bread were brushed with cigarette ash, like dirt engrained on the pores of a hand. To Anna's mind, it tilted the scene from wedding to funeral.

The only person in the room who bore the least resemblance to Don Giovanni—and that was only a second's illusion—was the manservant.

'I thought for a moment it must be your manservant.'

'Well why not?' Anne said.

'Why not? Did he seem—when you took him on—enterprising enough to put on a mask and try to seduce your guests?'

'No, I must confess. He seemed thoroughly reliable.'

'Well then.'

'Not here then?'

'Not here.'

'O dear,' Anne said. 'But Dr. Brompius *is* here. And alone.'

'Does that mean you've got to rescue him?'

'It's not', Anne said, 'unpromising. For you, I mean.'

Anna picked out the one person who was obviously alone. He stood, eating, beside the centre of the table: an elderly man, in ordinary evening dress, with a bulging belly, bulging eyes, bulging spectacles.

'Anne. It manifestly *is.*'

'No, darling,' said Anne. 'I won't let him kiss you. But he *is* a musicologist, you know.'

'I didn't,' said Anna, drawing her back. 'Or perhaps. Vaguely. I don't really *know* about these things.'

'Well you ought to,' said Anne. 'He's said to be immensely distinguished. He's working on Tom-Tom's collection. It's said to be an immense honour for us. Dr. Brompius, the distinguished Dutch musicologist?' she said, testing the formula. 'Or is he Swedish? I shall never understand why it's the least latin races that have the Latin ending for their names . . .'

'Do you think', Anna whispered, 'that in the accusative he's Dr. Brompium?'

'Docto*rem* Brompium,' Anne corrected, 'but do get out of your accusative frame of mind, darling.'

'You go,' said Anna, trying to detach her arm from Anne's. 'To adopt your own lousy pun, I'm not feeling very vocative.'

'I would rather not', said Anne, pulling her forward, 'be forced to examine which case *does* suit the way your thoughts are tending at the moment.' When they were half way across the room, Dr. Brompius looked up, and Anna had to stop tugging against the introduction.

Munching, he bowed to Anna; stopped munching while he kissed Anne's hand; and then went shamelessly on with the same mouthful, giving an indelicate impression that it was now a mouthful of Anne's hand through which he murmured to her, in a heavy unlatin accent:

'Chère madame.'

'Dr. Brompius,' Anne said, 'is it too much to consult you in your professional capacity a second time?'

'How could it be too much, chère madame, for you?'

But the gestures of Anne's head, referring always to Anna, made it clear that it was not for her but for Anna.

'Dr. Brompius', she explained to Anna, 'has already arranged some dance suites for us, for later in the evening.'

Dr. Brompius, taking the idea that he was to address himself to Anna, elaborated to her:

'Some little known works of the Swedish eighteenth-century court composers.'

Anna smiled at him, and sulked at Anne. But Anne went on:

'And now we want to consult you again. It's about Don *Giovanni*.'

'Ah, this is most interesting,' Dr. Brompius said. 'I will later explain why. But first you, chères mesdames.'

'We want to know', Anne said, 'whether Don Giovanni really does seduce Donna Anna.'

Anne refused absolutely to receive Anna's look. She fixed her eyes on Dr. Brompius, who said:

'This question is fascinating.'

'Of course we realise it's one of the classic puzzles. We know she says he didn't. But we know she'd have to *say* he didn't, in any case.'

'Here', said Dr. Brompius, 'is a question we must examine in its historical aspect.' He turned to the table and took a bridge roll. Now it was Anne who was trying to engage Anna's attention, and Anna who, now the thing was definitely started, had no better defence than to pretend to be insensitive to everything except a polite impatience for Dr. Brompius's reply. She fixed her gaze on the back of his head. When he turned round again—the bridge roll already, and whole, in his mouth—he took up Anna's gaze and held it.

'This question is one which we can answer, I think, without going into musical technicalities, which are so boring. What we, however, *must* consider is history. History is the thing with which we may not dispense. This was said by a professor whose lectures I have attended in Hamburg in 1909, a most gifted man, and I have never forgotten it. If we permit ourselves to forget that in dealing with this matter we are dealing not with a modern but with an eighteenth-century opera, dramatis personae, audience, librettist, etcetera, etcetera, we shall find that we are thinking unhistorically and we shall permit ourselves to be led astray. What we have to do in this case—chères mesdames, you are not eating.' He slid a silver dish from the table and thrust it towards Anna's waist. 'What we have to do is think our way into the conditions obtaining during the latter part of the eighteenth century, for that is when our opera was written, although, of course, its story is much older. To understand the opera situation at this period we must consider the whole culture-situation of the period, in which the opera-situation is embedded like a jewel in its setting.'

Anna looked down at the shallow silver dish he was

proffering. There was nothing in it except a paper doily, some strands of cress and a few crumbs of chopped hard-boiled egg.

She faintly shook her head, as though too rapt to attend to eating.

'You are not hungry,' said Dr. Brompius. 'In the light of the culture-situation of the period, let us examine the alternatives. Let us postulate, first, that Donna Anna has *not* been seduced. What, in these circumstances, will she say on this subject? She will say, I think, that she has not been seduced. For there is nothing in these circumstances, the circumstances of not having been seduced, which we are entitled to pick out from a psychological point of view as affording her a motive for telling a lie. We must now consider the other alternative. Let us suppose that Donna Anna *has* been seduced.'

At the edge of her vision Anna saw Anne give an apologetic signal to Dr. Brompius, a mime of being drawn away down the table perforce, of taking care nonetheless not to go out of earshot, of continuing at the very least to watch his lips, though she had against her will to slide further and further away, while her hand faintly trailed along the table top until by blindest chance it met a dish from which not all the bridge rolls had been taken.

'Now what is Donna Anna going to say if she in fact *has* been seduced? Two possibilities are open to her. This is in distinction from the former case, where we discovered that she was unlikely to say anything but the truth. In this present instance she *may*, as before, tell the truth. On the other hand, she may tell a lie. For in this instance, unlike the other, we may readily identify a motive which might prompt her to lie.'

Far down the table, Anne, with a bridge roll in her hand, was talking to a knot of guests.

Anna stared at Dr. Brompius's spectacles, which reminded her of the eye pieces of an antique gas mask.

'A woman in the eighteenth century who was known to have been seduced was considered dishonoured. Whether this was based upon any deep-seated moralistic or religious conviction need not concern us now. It is possible that the concept of dishonour was not in all strata of society taken wholly seriously. It may even have been regarded with a dash of cynicism, so typical of the period. For us, however, it is enough that this was the conventional belief, whether or not it was a real belief. For our purposes it is sufficient that it was believed to be believed. Here, then, we have Donna Anna's motive.'

Still distantly miming to Dr. Brompius that she was not doing, would not dream of doing, could not bear to do any such thing, Anne was leaving the room.

'When I refer to her motive, I mean, of course, her motive for lying—*if* she is lying. For let us consider the statement Donna Anna actually makes. She says —or, at least, the narrative she relates to Don Ottavio implies—that she has *not* been seduced. Now you will observe that this fulfils the requirements of at least one possibility in each of the alternatives we postulated. We postulated that if she had not been seduced she would say that she had not, and this is what in fact she does say. But we also postulated that if she *had* been seduced, it would be open to her to say that she had *not*, and this is again what she does in fact say or imply. In other words, we are not in a position to infer, on the basis of Donna Anna's own statement on the subject, from which of the two alternatives we postulated her motivation arises.'

To Anna's surprise, he stopped talking.

She waited, but he did not resume. He seemed to be waiting, rather, for her.

'Yes, I see,' she said in a thoughtful voice. 'But I'm afraid I still don't quite see the answer.'

'We have re-stated the problem', he said, 'in somewhat clearer terms.'

'O. Yes. I see.'

'And if you ask me how we can be sure that our new statement is somewhat clearer, that can be subjected to an empirical test. For from our new statement of the problem it emerges with greater clarity than it did before that it is not possible to infer the answer.'

'Yes,' said Anna.

'And you still will not take some food?' He put the dish back on the table. 'This seems to you perhaps an inconclusive answer?'

'Not at all.'

'The seeker after truth must sometimes accept inconclusive answers. This is better than to be misled.'

'Much better.'

'There is, however, one thing which we can state quite definitely and firmly, without fear of contradiction.'

'Is there?'

'Indeed there is. It is this. If Donna Anna had *not* been seduced, it is quite impossible—sociologically, historically and psychologically—*quite* impossible that she would ever have said that she *had.*'

'Unless she just liked mischief,' said Anna.

'O but I do not think she *did*,' said Dr. Brompius.

A third person joined them. Without difficulty, surprise or embarrassment, Anna recognised Don Giovanni.

Dr. Brompius took him in with a glance to the side and turned excitedly back to Anna.

'You will remember that I have said to you that it was very interesting that you should speak of this opera? This was because I already knew that this gentleman was here tonight in the character of Don Giovanni. Permit me to—'

'We've already met,' Don Giovanni said. 'I've come to claim Donna Anna.'

PART TWO

6

'You ran away,' he said.' Why?'

His black silken sleeve touched Anna's bare arm as they leaned on the parapet of the minstrels' gallery, looking down into the dancers.

'Lots of reasons. 'I'm old.'

'No older than I am.'

'Well I expect actually I *am*. But anyway isn't that one of the things that're said to be different for men?'

'It may be said. I shouldn't think it's particularly true.'

'If one wants to forget one's age,' Anna said, 'new year's eve is the wrong eve to start.'

'Tell me another of the reasons.'

'They're all interconnected. I'm no longer beautiful.'

He hesitated for an instant and then asked:

'Were you ever?'

She, too, considered before replying:

'Well, no. Obviously not, in that sense. But I must have had the sort of beauty that all young human beings have. Anyway, I must have turned into a horrible human being now', she added, 'because new year's eve fills me with thoughts against the young.'

He laughed. 'Don't think I don't know what you mean. It's a night for youthanasia.'

She turned to look at him, took the pun and said 'Yes', smiling. He bore no resemblance to the reconstruction she had made while she was searching for him; yet confronted with him her original memory responded to the summons and confirmed without hesitating that it was he and that she was perfectly well acquainted with what he looked like.

She even remembered, and quite precisely, that towards the wrist, where it fitted closely, his black sleeve wrinkled into small horizontal folds, like a sleeve by Watteau.

'Still,' he said, looking regretfully down at the dance floor, 'there's no need for violence. The youngest of them will grow old in time.'

'So I kept thinking,' Anna said. After a moment she added: 'You ran away, too.'

'No I didn't. I reculer-d pour mieux sauter.'

'*Where* did you reculer?'

'To the library.'

'O yes. I'd forgotten the library.'

'That doesn't surprise me,' he said. 'It's because you're not rich. *Are* you?'

'That's the second time I've been asked tonight. The other person was disappointed I wasn't.'

'I'd be disappointed if you were. I like the fellow feeling.

I could tell that you and I were both Cinderellas at this ball.'

'What has that to do with libraries?'

'O, because the rich have libraries, whereas people like us have books. People like us read books. The rich have them catalogued.'

'Anne reads them, I think.'

'I don't know about Anne. I'm fairly sure Tom-Tom doesn't.'

'Do you know Tom-Tom well?'

'Very well.' Presently he emended: 'Very well from one angle only—below. I work with him. At least, that's how he puts it, which is decent of him. In fact, I work *for* him.'

'We belong on different sides of the aisle,' Anna said. 'Bridegroom's party and bride's party.'

'But you don't work for Anne?'

'No.'

'What—'

'Were you in the library the whole time?' Anna asked.

'Yes, from the moment you ran away. I found old Grumpius or whatever he's called in there.'

'No doubt he's got in the habit of being in there. He's been working on Tom-Tom's musicological things. Tom-Tom collects manuscript scores and so forth.'

'So Grumpius told me, but at greater length. Fortunately, he got hungry after a while. But it's just as well he

77

was in there, because he's arranged everything according to some system, with the result that you can't find anything without his help. Anyway, why, in particular? I mean about where I was?'

'No reason in particular,' Anna said. 'What were you looking for?'

'Evidence. To convince you it's no use running away.'

'Did you find it?'

He handed her a piece of paper, which she unfolded. It was die-stamped at the top with Anne's and Tom-Tom's address. Underneath, Don Giovanni had copied out in pencil: —

'. . . what is true is that she is one of the hero's victims, that Don Giovanni in the dark of night, disguised as Don Ottavio, has reached the summit of his desires, and that the curtain rises at the moment when Donna Anna has come to the realization of the terrible truth of her betrayal. In the eighteenth century no one misunderstood this. It goes without saying that in the famous recitativo accompagnato *in which she designates Don Giovanni to her betrothed as the murderer of her father, she cannot tell Don Ottavio the whole truth . . .'*

Underneath he had written:

'Einstein, Mozart, *p. 439'*

Anna handed the paper back to him. 'In all the authorities you must have consulted, could you find only one to back you up?'

'But what an authority,' he said, putting the paper away in the pocket of his eighteenth-century coat. '*The* authority.'

'Incidentally,' Anna said, 'you can't kill my father. He's been dead for ten years.'

'It's not that aspect of my character I'm pursuing tonight.'

'Yet it's that aspect that's preoccupying me tonight.'

'Of my character?'

'No, of things in general. It comes between me and your character. No doubt it's really why I ran away.'

They were silent for a moment. Anna shifted her stance a little, so that her wrist instead of her elbows rested on the parapet and she was no longer touching Don Giovanni. She clasped her hands. She was aware of Don Giovanni's gaze moving slightly sideways, towards her: not enough to take in *her*, but taking in her hands and, probably, her wedding ring.

'Seriously,' he said, 'if that's so, it's all the more reason for you *not* to run away.'

She did nothing.

She felt him move. One arm remained extended, the hand lying on the parapet, but he had shifted round to stand behind her, perhaps in order to come in contact with her again—her back could faintly feel him —or per-haps in order to speak from behind, with the voice of a tempter.

'There's only one answer to thoughts of that kind,' he said from behind her.

She did not reply.

'Seriously. It's a well-known psychological fact. Obses-sive thoughts about death are in inverse proportion to the frequency of sexual intercourse.'

She made no move.

'Listen,' he said in a rough voice. 'How long is it? When did you last have an affair?'

For a moment it appeared she was still not going to answer. Then she turned completely round, leaned her back against the parapet and stared full at him, deep into his mask.

'Last year,' she said, making her own face like a mask.

'O, but tonight,' he said quickly, '*tonight* that could mean . . .'

'Yes,' said Anna. She stared at him an instant longer and then turned again and gazed deep into the dancing.

It had become intense. Some of the lights had been turned out. Frills of talk and laughter from the verges of the ballroom and from the more brightly lit corridors and rooms round it indicated that those people who danced only socially were pursuing their social purposes else-where and had withdrawn from the dance floor, leaving only couples who were seriously interested either in dancing or in one another. The band itself was playing less noisily and more intently, giving only a concentration of its musical purpose, which would be understandable to connoisseurs.

Don Giovanni moved away from Anna: she was aware he had moved further along, into the recess of the gallery, the small, dark, dusty section at the end, which was invisible to the ballroom.

Few of the dancers spoke to one another. The band had almost abnegated melody. For bars at a stretch the only sound it made was a dry bean-bag noise, as though seeds were being shaken inside a gourd. From the floor the only sound was a concerted shuffling of feet, like a rhythmical breathless sighing, or like the repeated sifting of brown sugar with a spoon held by someone concentrating on something else.

Don Giovanni came back to her. 'Did you know there was a curtain here?'

'A curtain?'

They spoke in low voices, because of the quiet in the ballroom.

Anna followed him along to the end of the gallery. Drawn well back, bunched up and stowed out of sight was an immense heavy curtain of a patterned deep yellow brocade which brought to mind the word *genoese*.

'Tom-Tom and Anne must have been having amateur

theatricals up here,' Don Giovanni said.

He took a handful of the curtain and gave it a tug. It ran easily along the rail at the top: its rings, which must have been horn, not brass, made a rattling like the ribs of a fan or of a peacock's tail. Dust fell out of the material. Anna gave a slight cough.

Taking a great swathe of the curtain, Don Giovanni enveloped himself and Anna. 'Now we're really in the opera house. We've got a box.'

She pushed a fold in the edge of the curtain and held it down, so that she could see out. He, further into the recess and deeper in curtain, was not even pretending.

At the far end of the ballroom the egg-shaped man was walking towards the double doors as though to open them and leave the ball. But dancers came between him and Anna and she could not see whether he really did or not.

Muffled beneath the curtain, Don Giovanni's arm fell like the shadow of a branch in spring sunshine across Anna's back. His hand, making itself into the shape of a prehensile flower with five fleshy petals, settled round her breast. She moved neither towards him nor away from him. His head bent towards the side of her neck; she felt the velvet, accidental contact of his mask before she felt the searching contact of his lips. After a moment she said 'No'. She still had not moved, but the very fact that her flesh did not yield made an impression as though she was pulling against him. His lips nuzzled for a moment more at her neck. Then he let her go and moved a little apart.

Ruth Blumenbaum was almost without thoughts. She could perceive only a distant glimmer of thought, which she knew to be dread of the ending of the dance. For the time being she and Edward were one in the near-absence of thought: a telepathy of having nothing to communicate. He was dancing with her not in his usual loose and lively way but close to. Heat generated between them fused them like a couple sharing a fireside: an aged peasant couple, in a long, an almost unending, a medieval winter's night. His sweating cheek was pressed against hers as though they could never come unstuck. The two cheeks might have been two fragments of broken china, reunited, being held together for the glue to set. The bristles on his jaw ate into her skin, on the verge of becoming painful to her but never quite crossing the verge, preventing her, rather, from ever quite crossing the verge into complete automatism: they caught at her interest because only men's faces had them; and the physical sense of them was a sub-pleasure to her, a sub-stimulus; they were minute hooks, sub-erotic, tattoo needles, hundreds of little grapples holding her to him. Through his thin silk costume she could feel his warmth and sweat and the actual outline of his breasts. Her white silk thighs moved in perfect accord with his black silk thighs—so perfect that they hardly moved, were hardly voluntarily controlled, but had become automatic fins swishing to hold the two of them steady in the stream. Yet she was afraid of Edward's rebellion against all this when the music should stop.

'You're not afraid of being a bitch, are you?'

'Not particularly,' said Anna.

'Why not?'

'Why should I be? I've experienced frustrated desire. That's one of the things I *don't* believe are different for men.'

'You mean you've experienced it and it wasn't so bad?'

'O, bad,' she said and shrugged. 'It's bearable.'

'Well anything's bearable', he said, 'that people have to bear. That's a poor argument. That would justify anything.' His voice was churlish and resentful, on purpose.

The music stopped. The extra lights were switched on again. The band began to play something jolly. The sound, going out through the house, began to attract more people to the floor.

'This is more like us,' Edward said. He took Ruth by the hand only to fling her away from him. 'Come on, let's whoop this party up some.'

'Well. What shall we talk about now?' Don Giovanni said, in a bitter voice. He took the curtain, which was now wholly in his possession, folded it into a roll and shaped it into a yoke round his neck, like a commedia dell'arte character feigning hanging himself. 'Shall I tell you the story of my life?'

'Let's preserve our anonymity,' Anna said. 'At least.'

'Meaning that's all we've got left?'

'Well that's something,' she said, '—something romantic'; and then, going back to reply to his question: 'Meaning what more would we really know if we did know all about each other?'

'Have you noticed what a metaphysical ball this is?' he said. 'All these people bumping into one another and asking "Who are you?" even when they've known each other for years.'

'You see,' said Anna.

'What's the psychology of costume balls?' he casually asked.

'I don't know. I've never been to one before.'

'Neither have I.'

'I don't know,' she repeated. 'Dressing up, perhaps? Everyone loves to dress up? At least, children do.'

'Since I ceased to be a child I've preferred undressing.'

'O you should have come naked,' she said, rather sarcastically and impatiently. 'Then everyone would have known you were Don Giovanni at first glance.'

'Well it's only make-believe either way, as you've impressed on me. 'I'm not an emperor and I wasn't invited to take off my new clothes.'

'What difference would it have made, in the long run?'

'O, none, I suppose,' he said ironically. 'But I was thinking of the short run.'

'Then we were bound to be out of step, as I can't get my mind off the long run.'

'Rudy, darling,' said Myra Blumenbaum, in her gentle, failing, lady-like voice, 'you're out of time.'

'Out of time with you,' he said in his chipper voice, 'but in time with the music.'

'O,' she said, sounding hurt. 'Perhaps that's true.' But then she usually did sound hurt, even when she wasn't.

'Now that I'm not going to cuckold him, I feel you owe me some information about your husband. Or has he been dead for ten years, too?'

They were again leaning on the parapet, arm parallel with arm, cheek parallel with cheek; but not touching. Anna had let her clasped hands drop, from the wrists, below the level of the parapet, but not out of Don Giovanni's sight. She was aware of his head turned ten degrees from the straight and of his gaze resting, consumingly, on her hands.

'My husband——' she began, but broke off. She twisted her wedding ring a millimetre further round. '*Please* let's remain anonymous.'

'All right. But it restricts the conversation.'

'It needn't. Tell me what sort of person you are. In general terms.'

'I don't think in general terms.'

'What things do you think about?'

'Mozart and sex,' he said.

'Nothing else?'

'Nothing else in general terms. And you?'

'Mozart, sex and death,' she said.

There was a pause. They both burst into laughter.

'What made you come to this costume ball', he presently asked, 'since you don't usually go to them?'

'To please Anne, I suppose. No. I'm fond enough of Anne to displease her if I want to. Because it was eighteenth-century, probably.'

'Because of Mozart?'

'I daresay. And you?'

'O, I've never been *asked* to one before. But I probably wouldn't have gone, for any other century.'

'What's the psychology of historical costume balls?' she asked.

'I don't know. One's childhood, I suppose,' he said. 'Most things are. I really came', he added, 'because I wanted to see the house. I've never been here before.'

'I came to see the house filled with eighteenth-century people. But of course they don't, subtly, look right.'

'It's the faces,' he said.

'Fake faces . . . You think they'll pass, and then at the last

87

minute they won't. Just as mine won't pass for seventeen.'

'I don't see why you should want it to,' he said.

'You had the sense to hide yours. It's easy to say that from behind a mask.'

'Shall I take it off?' He put his hand to it.

'No,' she said quickly. He lowered his hand. 'I might know you,' she said.

'I promise you you don't. At least, I don't know you. You needn't be afraid that I am actually your husband. Or your brother or your uncle.'

'What an operatic world you must think I live in', she said, 'where to disguise the upper part of the face is to disguise all, and women are never surprised that the man they married as a baritone has turned into a tenor overnight, or even a soprano.'

'Perhaps opera heroines are tone deaf.'

'Well, some singers, of course . . .'

'When we next meet, I shan't be in the mask. Shall you know me?'

'We shan't meet.'

'How can you be sure?'

'I can't be sure. But the chances are about as small as the chances of committing incest by taking up with a masked stranger.'

'The chances of that depend on the size of one's family.'

She laughed. 'And our meeting again depends on the

size of the gathering. Don't you see, it's taken a really big do, Tom-Tom's net and Anne's net both cast really wide, to bring us together *once*? Do you like the house, by the way, now that you see it?'

'I'd seen the outside. I knew it would be pretty. But actually, the inside—it's pretty, but' I'm disappointed. It doesn't satisfy my historical sense. Is it too done up? Faked?'

'Or not faked enough?'

'How do you mean?'

'Well, since they're rich, most of their pieces *are* eighteenth-century. So they look a bit battered. Presumably in the eighteenth century things didn't *look* two hundred years old.'

'Yes, maybe it's that,' he said. He turned round, so that his back was to the parapet. 'Surely you wouldn't want to be seventeen again?'

'Your mask doesn't hide your train of thought,' Anna said.

'That wasn't my train of thought.' He turned back towards the ballroom again, and lowered his head. The mask did not hide a slight blush either.

'I don't want to *be* seventeen,' Anna said, more gently, 'only to be capable of passing for it.'

'I think that's a mistaken wish,' he muttered. After gazing down on the ball for a minute he said: 'All preoccupation with history is preoccupation with one's own past. The unanswerable question:– what was it like to live then?

89

But of course living in 1787 wasn't *like* anything, any more than being seventeen was, or being seven. They were just living and being.'

'All the same. Twentieth-century faces *are* different.'

'Yes, they give the show away.' He looked at her sideways. 'You blame the faces for being twentieth-century, and the furniture for not being.'

'Why shouldn't I? Life isn't arranged moralistically. It isn't *fair.*'

'No. It's certainly not that.'

'Actually, the prettiest room in this house is almost completely fake,' Anna said. 'Anne's bedroom.'

'O. Well naturally I haven't seen that.'

'No more than I've seen the office where Tom-Tom works. Though I suppose I *could* see that, if I wanted to.'

'No reason why you should want to. There's nothing pretty in Tom-Tom's office.'

'There's nothing ugly in Anne's bedroom . . . Even so, you mightn't like the effect. You might say it was tart's rococo. It isn't,' she corrected. 'I feel disloyal for even suggesting it . . .' She corrected herself again: 'No, I don't. It *is* tart's rococo. But I adore it.'

'You make it sound very enticing,' he said.

'It is. Like sugar. Like peppermint creams.'

'Funny thing,' Edward said, coming in close enough to Ruth to talk to her but still panting from the strenuous steps he had been performing on his own, 'when I was dancing with whatshername—*that woman*—someone up in that gallery place threw down a lot of peppermint creams.'

His head alluded illustratively up to the gallery. Ruth's gaze followed his gesture.

'She's up there now,' Ruth said.

'Who is?'

'Anna. With a man.'

He turned to look, and then went on dancing. 'I can't understand how anyone would *want* to spend the evening just watching other people dance.'

'I expect Anna's too old to do much dancing,' said Ruth.

'O I don't know,' Edward said. 'Look at the way your father's been hopping around like a grasshopper all night.'

'Yes, but Daddy isn't *like* an old person. Mummy hasn't danced much. And only with Daddy.'

'I expect Anna whatsit went up there to cuddle her man,' Edward said. 'But it's a damn silly place to choose. They can't have sex up there with everyone looking.'

He had danced Ruth down towards the end of the ballroom, near the gallery. He looked up, waited his chance and caught Anna's eye. He threw her a kiss.

She waved back.

'Who's that?' Don Giovanni asked.

'I don't know his real name. For tonight he's Casanova.'

9 1

'What a young Casanova.'

'The girl, whose real name I *do* know, is Cherubino.'

'The funny thing is, although she's so dark and he's so fair, they look alike.'

'It's their common youth.'

'And of course they're dressed alike. One black, one white.'

'The fair one in black, and the dark one in white.'

'They look almost like brother and sister,' said Don Giovanni, watching them dance back into the crowd and lose themselves. 'Or I suppose I should say brother and brother.'

'Your mind runs on incest,' said Anna.

'Anne, dearie. Lovely dress. Lamé, isn't it?'

'Rudy, dear friend.'

'Lovely party, too, dear.'

'I'm so glad if you're enjoying it.'

'O we are. You do know Myra, don't you?'

'Yes of course. We've often met'——and never found anything to say.

Anne and Myra smiled at one another and prolonged the smiles. Rudy seemed unable to break the silence of his wife. Anne considered putting the obvious question who Myra was, but it was answered before put by the obvious fact that she was nothing—nothing except Myra. Her costume was simply one of Myra's usual evening dresses—one of Myra's usual evening gowns: draped dove-grey crêpe, chosen for its inability to make any noise, even if you violently shook it, which Myra would never do—or encourage anyone else to do: chosen at great cost to make as nearly as possible the effect of not being there and yet remaining at the furthest possible remove from leaving Myra naked. At last Anne said to her:

'Ruth looks sweet as Cherubino'

and at the same moment Rudy said to Anne:

'Spare me a dance, Anne dear?'

'O I'd love to, Rudy, but I mustn't. You haven't seen Anna, have you?'

'Anna? I had a dance with her earlier. We were cut in on.'

'I *must* find her. I want to make sure she's all right. I did such an awful thing to her.'

'I can't believe that,' Rudy said. 'I thought you two were as thick as thieves.'

'O my dear,' said Anne, 'you make me feel all the more remorseful. I must find her. I left her ententacled. By a sort of octopus. He always reminds me of an octopus. He *bulges* so. Well my dear, I know I bulge myself. I may remind people of an octopus myself. But he's so hungry. I'm afraid he may have eaten her . . .'

Anne oozed away from them; and when she had gone Myra said, in a soft, worried and completely serious voice:

'O Rudy. How *awful* for Anna.'

*

'Was it a peppermint cream', Ruth abruptly asked Edward, 'that she was *feeding* you? I mean, practically from her own mouth?'

'Were you there? I thought you were doing your diary.'

'I came back.'

'O.'

'Did you actually *eat* it?' Ruth said. 'How *could* you?'

'Well of course I ate it. What the hell else would I do with a peppermint cream?'

'Casanova was at the first performance of *Don Giovanni*. The real Casanova, I mean, Did you know that?'

'Yes, actually,' Anna replied, without much emphasis. 'The first performance was on the twenty-ninth of October, 1787.'

'Good God. How did you remember that?'

'Well, you can remember, too. The year, anyway.'

'Can I? Anyway, how do you know I can?'

'Because you said living in 1787 wouldn't be *like* anything.'

'Did I? I didn't really notice I did. I mean, I didn't pick on the year consciously. But, anyway, I've just been going through the reference books. You must have it all in your head.'

'It isn't really miraculous,' Anna said. 'For one thing, I once did some research on Don *Giovanni*—'

'Did you publish it?' he interrupted quickly. 'I'll read it.'

'It's under my maiden name.'

'That doesn't impress *me* as an obstacle. You're forgetting I don't even know your married name. And *were* you a maiden when you published it?'

'It *is* a long time ago, but not so long as that.'

'When—'

'And for another thing,' Anna said, 'I have the sort of mind that remembers numbers.'

'Some numbers, like your age, you seem unable to forget.'

'You're quite right,' she said, turning her head and looking at him for a moment. 'It isn't a gift. I mean, it's not enviable.'

'But you have other gifts. For example, you're musical.'

'Fairly,' she said. 'Nothing exceptional.'

'I think I'd better not say what I think your other gifts are. I might make you angry.'

'O then don't,' Anna said. After a pause, she added: 'Actually, I *have* one other gift, which you don't know about.'

'Are you going to demonstrate it to me?'

'I can't, with so many people here. I don't', she added, 'mean *that*.'

But he laughed—with pleasure.

'You haven't seen Anna, have you?'

'Not for ages,' said Lady Hamilton. 'She's been disappearing all night.'

'O dear. Excuse me, dear.'

'Anne!' Lady Hamilton ran after her. 'I've been looking for *you*. I want to thank you.'

'You're not leaving?'

'I must. I'm dropping with exhaustion.'

'Stay for the cabaret. It'll be quite soon.'

'*Dropping.* With *exhaustion.*'

'O dear. How sad,' said Anne.

'Good night. I hope you find Anna,' Lady Hamilton said, reading where Anne's thoughts really were.

'Where did they get the chandeliers?' Don Giovanni asked.

'Anne got them. From an eighteenth-century house in Dublin, that was being sold up.'

There were three chandeliers. They marched straight down the middle of the pretty stuccoed ceiling, dividing the ballroom into three calm, magnificent bays. They were not illuminated, because Anne had refused to spoil them by having them wired; but the electric lights struck sparks from them.

'I often wish I was big enough to wear them,' Anna said.

'You'd be a monster. You'd need three ears.'

Anne looked into the library, saw Dr. Brompius there alone, was reminded of a monster, framed the thought 'Dr. Octopus' and shut the door again.

*

'Each one,' Don Giovanni said, 'reminds me of an immensely ornate aria for a Mozart soprano. It's the way each piece of glass just drops into space, like a note. Those sort of glass necklaces that are draped from one branch to the next are the runs. And of course the actual glitter, the fire, is pure coloratura.'

'They *can* sing, as a matter of fact,' Anna said.

'You mean they tinkle, if there's a wind? Or if you could get up there to give them a shake?'

'Yes, they do that, but they also perform spontaneously. They vibrate in sympathy, if you choose the right note to set them off.'

'Is it known what note?'

'An A natural.'

'A for Anne, of course?'

'Of course. I'd demonstrate, if the people weren't here.'

'I hope you'd get it right first time. I'd hate your demonstration to fall flat.'

'O, I'd get it right. I wouldn't offer to demonstrate otherwise.' She paused and then said: 'I've got perfect pitch.'

'That's your other gift?'

She turned sideways, leaning her hip on the parapet, and looked direct at his profile. 'My only gift.'

He turned to face her. He stood, one hand on the parapet, one leg loosely crossed in front of the other; tightly, ripplingly black-silk-costumed; thin, largeish, rather elegant, relaxed: Harlequin. From his mask he half appraised, half challenged her. In the end he said: 'I think that's absolutely perfect.'

'Yes, well it *is*. Perfect,' she said, without dropping her eyes.

'I don't just mean the pitch. I mean perfect for you.'

'I know you do . . . It's just a complete, perfect, isolated gift,' she said. 'I *am* fairly musical, but it's got nothing to do with that. It's detached. It's no good to anyone or anything. There's nothing you can do by, with or from it, except tune pianos. There's nothing you can do about it. It's slightly fantastic and quite irrelevant. It's like the form of some exotic marine creature that's not only very low on the scale of being but quite out of the main course of evolution. It's simply there. It's perfect: but why?'

'You'd think she was more *experienced*', Edward said,' than to go somewhere where everyone can see.'

7

'I had to run away,' Anna said. 'It was the only thing to do.'

'Was it?'

'You don't understand?'

'Well naturally you can't expect it to look the same from my point of view.'

'Well at least it was *something* to do. I mean, it was something to *do*. There's nothing worse than just waiting passively for things to be done.'

'Yes, well that I do understand, in a way,' he said. 'I've often thought that must be one of the difficulties about being a woman.'

'It's not really even about being a woman. It happens to whichever isn't the active one. I mean, the woman can make the advances. I have done, in my time. But then you only put the man in the intolerable position. It's like being a patient, and waiting for them to do things to you. Or like being an actor and having nothing to do with your hands. It would be much easier to be asked to do something very difficult with them.'

'All the same', he said, 'it's not always easy and straightforward being the active one.'

'No, of course not.'

'You may miscalculate. You may overshoot the mark.'

'Yes.'

'As I did.' He gave her a brief look.

'Yes.' She didn't look at him. 'Did you come as Don Giovanni', she asked, 'with a view to finding someone to seduce?'

He hesitated before replying:

'I don't know whether you'll find this flattering or the opposite. But, actually, no. That aspect of the character— though it's really the obvious one—didn't really strike me until I met you. I was thinking more of Don Giovanni as the social rebel.'

'Are you a social rebel?'

'Well, more a social outcast. It would be truer to say society kicked me out than that I kicked against it. It's not prepared to pay me to do the things I like doing, which are mainly quite passive and useless, like listening to Mozart, and so I have to do a job which I think is quite useless but which society calls doing an honest day's work.'

'There's no *class* that cares about Mozart,' she said.

'No.'

'There never has been. When he was working for the Archbishop of Salzburg, his place at table was with the servants. Above the cooks, but below the valets.'

'On nights like this, I hate the rich,' he said.

'Yes.'

'Almost as much as I hate the poor.'

'Yes. I see. You *are* an outcast.'

'Aren't you?'

Instead of replying, she said, as she looked down at the dancers:

'Earlier this evening I felt as though I knew what everyone in the room was thinking. Now I feel I don't know what *any* of them are. They're all so frankly here for pleasure. I can't think why it doesn't embarrass them.'

'Why should it embarrass them?'

'This passivity, again,' she said. 'If I say to myself "Now I'm setting out to seek pleasure", my mind goes blank. I don't know what to do with my hands. One of the bravest things about the eighteenth century was that people were always frankly setting off on pleasure parties.'

'O, that was part of the aristocratic frame of mind,' he said, 'which no longer exists. Nowadays it's all so sordid. The first thing Tom-Tom does when he gets to the office every morning is search *The Times* to make sure his shares haven't dropped. Well, I *mean*. He might as well take his socks off to make sure his arches haven't. It's the sort of thing aristocrats didn't do.'

'O I don't know,' she said. 'I doubt if the aristocratic frame of mind ever existed.'

'I always thought it did until the French Revolution.'

'And yet even before the French Revolution each work of art contained a French Revolution. Each great work of art, I mean.'

'It's a very impressive remark,' he said.

'It may even be true,' she said. 'When Don Giovanni gave a pleasure party it ended in the Terror. A statue came to supper and hauled him off to Hell.'

'You're going a long way towards justifying your remark.'

'And then', she said, 'those people going on pleasure parties in Watteau's pictures, in those beautiful boats that look like rococo beds. Or *Così,* which is one enormous pleasure party.'

'Yes? What about them?'

'Well, they're so *sad,*' she said. 'Those are tragic works of art.'

'O, that's because people have to die,' he said. 'Pleasure has to end *then.*'

'I thought', she said, 'it was you who were reproaching me for that thought.'

'Damn,' he said.

She laughed.

'Nevertheless,' he said. 'Nevertheless, I do reproach you. It's a thought that must be overcome.'

'You've already given me your prescription.'

'I'd like to emend it.'

'All right. Emend it.'

'The prescription is simply "Be brave". That's the moral of *Don Giovanni.* He was the bravest man in the world. Death is coming. All right, it's coming. Whatever happens, one mustn't let it browbeat one into believing in God and the Devil.'

'You don't?' she asked.

'No. Do you?'

'No.'

'I just can't', he said, with an effect of helplessness, 'see it in the same way as other people seem to. Or as they say they do. Or let it be thought they do.'

'What way, in particular?'

'Well the people down there', he began, nodding towards them fiercely, 'or at least about half of them, including most of the older ones, would consider most of the things I consider thoroughly desirable, like seducing you, either wrong or silly. Silly because there's no money in it. Whereas a good deal of what they do for a living and almost everything they do for pleasure seems to me criminal.'

'For example?'

'For example—o, killing animals.'

'I, too', Anna said carefully, after watching her wrist bones for a moment while she turned them this way and that, 'find it easier to like animals than people. And things than animals.'

'I can't go with you as far as the things,' he said.

'You're not as old as I am. That's the remark that used to make one livid at seventeen. Isn't it odd one should have lived to make it oneself? Your prescription, by the way, seems too passive to me.'

'Would you rather revert to the earlier one?'

'No.'

'And yet', he said, 'even though you didn't want to wait for it passively, you nearly took the earlier one, didn't you?'

'Nearly,' she admitted. 'It had the appeal of iconoclasm. I was hating the rich tonight, too. It attracted me because middle-aged, middle-class women just *don't*. With masked men in the middle of the night,' she added.

'They still don't, you know,' he said, opening up an invitation by tilting his head and glancing at her sideways.

She shook her head.

'You can't be brave passively,' she said. 'Hence the guillotine. I think Don Giovanni was perfectly right to go round seducing women until he provoked Hell into coming to get him prematurely. I shan't wait to die, either.'

'Do you mean you'll forestall it?'

'Yes. Then at least I shan't have it done to me. Since it must be done, I'll do it. Like taking the sticking plaster off for oneself.' In a faintly sardonic voice she added: 'Don't worry—I'm not going to do it tonight. Not for some considerable time. Not middle-age-anasia. Just one day before it can do it to me.'

'You're perfectly serious, aren't you?'

'Perfectly,' she said frivolously, 'but I *couldn't* choose tonight. It would *ruin* Anne's party.'

'You won't be able to do it at all.'

'Why not—if I don't spoil any party? Myself is the only person I'm prepared to injure. Injuring others involves too much responsibility.'

'You obviously *are* involved with people,' he said. 'You can make yourself anonymous to me, but you can't have spent your whole life at a costume ball. There must *be* people who know you and love you, and whom you love. And that's why you'll find you can't do it.'

'Sometimes I think I don't love anyone except Anne. And I'm feeling a bit cross with *her* at the moment.'

'Are you in love with Anne, perhaps?' he suggested.

'No, it's more as though we were mother and daughter.'

'". . . and, as Leda, was the mother of Helen of Troy, and, as Saint Anne, the mother of Mary."'

'What's that?'

'Walter Pater.'

'O yes, of course: "She is older than the rocks among which she sits." O my *dear*,' Anna said, 'I don't like your trains of thought.'

He put up both hands to cover his ears. 'Stop beating me about the head with trains of thought. As a matter of fact, that's a favourite incantation of mine. I often murmur it in times of trouble.'

'Is this a time of trouble?'

'Of course. You're very troubling.'

'Well, think', she said gaily,' how much worse it would be for Anne's party if I died in the middle of it *in*voluntarily.'

'I don't want to think of it at all.'

'"Be brave",' she mocked. 'I suppose', she added, 'that a man with the name of Pater would *have* to have an obsession with mothers.'

'*Your* mind runs on incest,' he said.

'It is quite true', she said, 'that it's the idea of *mother*—of having one or being one—that's always betraying me.'

'How do you mean, betraying?'

'It prevents me from being perfect. It brings my plans for being perfect to nothing. I'm one of the people who would like to be perfect.'

'Shouldn't we all?'

'No, some people prefer life to perfection, I think. And take imperfection as a sign of life. Whereas I should like to be complete, even at the risk of being cut off. I rather like the inorganic. Or at least the not very highly organic. No doubt I feel safer with them. Ideally, I would live surrounded by very beautiful, highly coloured, fantastic reptiles or fish. Something cold-blooded, that had never been in a womb— that had never even been properly hatched. Birds are too nearly like mammals, because the eggs are sat on. Cold-blooded creatures wouldn't try to have any sort of relationship with me, wouldn't even recognise me, and so I shouldn't feel sad when they died. They could just turn their bellies up and float up to the top of tank. And I'd throw the corpse in the dustbin and buy a new one.'

'Well, why *don't* you live surrounded by fish?' he said, in a depressed voice.

'Because mammals exist, I suppose.'

For some time they stood in silence, listening to the music from below, which presently changed into a syrupy waltz—to accompany which some of the lights were turned out again.

Anna said quietly and rather rapidly:

'Damned little furry, warm-blooded, cuddly mammals, always wanting to know what you're thinking, whether you're going to cuddle them or give them their dinner—if they're very young, they're always nuzzling around to find your breasts if you're a woman. They're almost as bad as people. They and I have only to take one look at each other and one or other of us starts *comforting* the other. They have the same aspiration to immortal souls as people, but of course there are only mortal souls, and so one dreads their death. And so there's remorse. There's a Siamese kitten up in Anne's bedroom at this moment which I feel remorseful towards, because I wasn't very nice to it. I mean, I *didn't* comfort it. Siamese cats seem to me so reptilian that I think I can treat them as reptiles. But of course they're mortals, mammals, like anyone else. It wants mothering. Anne mothers it. It's allowed to lie on her bed. Perhaps I was jealous of it, for that reason. It has an image of Anne. All mammals form images of you, and so you feel remorse, because you *can't* live up to the image.'

'Why shouldn't you?' he asked in a hostile voice. 'Why shouldn't someone live up to the image, for once?'

'Because what people want the image to have is immortality. Sometimes they even want the image to confer it, as well.'

He began to protest.

'Didn't you', she asked, 'try to sell me sexual intercourse as a prescription against thoughts of death?'

'It was you that had the thoughts. That's not what I wanted it for.'

'You wanted some sort of comfort from me.' She confessed quickly, so that he should not feel obliged to contradict: 'And I from you. But mothers can't prevent children from dying, or children mothers, or lovers lovers. I can't even make a Siamese kitten immortal. We're doomed to disappoint one another. Everyone, I mean. Everyone all round.'

In a rather fatigued voice he asked:

'Did you run away because you were afraid of disappointing me?'

'At first,' she said, not replying to the question, 'our thoughts did pursue the same course, even though we were apart. You guessed I'd be debating whether Donna Anna really was seduced or not.'

'But later our thoughts diverged? Well, you've only yourself to blame. It was you that ran away. You can't expect everything of telepathy. After a bit the lines of communication get over-extended. At least, it always feels like telepathy, doesn't it? But what I really mean is that if you don't know very much about a person you've only a certain amount of material out of which to supply their thoughts.'

'I didn't say I had anyone else to blame. I think I'm probably to blame for the whole mistake.'

'When did you decide it *was* a mistake?'

'When you made love to me, it felt to me like a put-up job. As though you were fulfilling a napoleonic masterplan, rather than actually being attracted by *me*. Had you, in fact, been standing in the library telling yourself you could carry it off, you were Superman, you were the great seducer?'

'Not exactly,' he said. 'But if I thought more about what I'd like to be than what you really were—well, you'd removed yourself from view.'

'I had the same feeling of a put-up job when you called me a bitch.'

'It is possible', he cautiously admitted, 'that I squealed rather louder about that than I'd actually been hurt.'

'I'm just not', she said, making her voice comically rueful, 'as attractive as I'd supposed.'

The music in the ballroom came to a stop and was replaced by chatter.

'Obviously,' Don Giovanni said, 'I can't say anything to contradict that—*now*. The whole situation is a minefield. I'm not sure which of us mined it. But I think I'd better just stand still for a bit and not move an inch either way.'

Presently Anna said, raising her voice slightly to surmount the chattering from below:

'I'd like to be attractive not as a person but as a thing. Not to be made use of—no monetary value: I'd like to be a useless thing. I'd like to be neither warm-blooded nor cold-blooded but just for there to be no question of blood at all. Nobody would worry if I was alive or dead providing I was made of something that had never been either. Of course, I should like to be an ornamental thing, but not a work of art, because people feel remorse towards those and guilt if they let them be destroyed, so simply a work of craft, a decoration, something very contrived, very highly wrought, that wouldn't touch the heart at all . . .'

'If it's any consolation,' he said after a moment, 'though you're not in the least beautiful, you're the most ornamental person I've ever met.'

'Thank you.'

He stopped leaning on the parapet, stood up straight and brushed the dust—if there was any—off the front of his costume. 'Where does all this get us?'

'Nowhere.'

'Wouldn't we do better to go and seek pleasure, even if it does embarrass you a little?'

'Yes,' she said, standing up straight, too. 'Shall we go down and dance?'

'Yes.'

He opened the small door in the gallery wall. Behind them in the ballroom all the lights went out.

'What's happening now?'

They groped forward to the parapet and peered into the ballroom, where the people had been struck with silence in the dark. Here and there a giggle flared up and then went out, like a match. In one corner someone did light a match. It went out,

A single steel-blue spotlight came on, felt round among the people, mowing swathes through them like machine gun fire, and quickly focused on the shallow wooden platform where the band had been but which was now empty apart from the piano and a double bass leaning against the piano stool. The blue light blanched the wooden boards of the platform until they looked like wood turned to ash,

'I think it's going to be the cabaret,' Anna said,

'Damn,' he said. 'We'd better stay up here for a bit.'

8

As soon as the spotlight established itself, the people were reassured, even though it was not they it was illuminating. Without waiting to see who was going to step into the light, they filled the ballroom with talk again.

The person who did, from somewhere in the surrounding dark, step up on to the platform was Tom-Tom.

To Anna's eyes, in the minstrels' gallery, he presented only his back, but it was an unmistakable, characteristic back: huge, even when seen from above, and shapeless—shape-defying: his dark blue eighteenth-century silk costume became on him a dishevelled dressing gown. Naturally, there *was* no cord round the waist, and yet he seemed to be loosely lumped and knotted together by one; he turned the ball into a late, frowsty breakfast.

Coming from above, the spotlight broke on Tom-Tom's head, illuminating for most people in the ballroom his face but for Anna the back of his neck, which ran in folds, again without shape, this way and that. At the most brilliant point of illumination, the light reported colours truthfully. It shewed Tom-Tom's neck as the deep ochre tinged with russet which Anna knew it really to be—the out-of-doors colour one would expect to see on a gardener or, which Tom-Tom was at weekends, sailor. He spent as many weekends as he could in his sailing dinghy: a huge, clumsy-footed man in a small, delicate boat that could be pierced by a clumsily placed foot: alone in it, because even gentle sailing in a harbour, which was all Tom-Tom did, made Anne sea-sick. Anna imagined that his manoeuvres within the harbour walls must consist of keeping his back to the sun, because his face and the front of his neck were quite white and city-looking. The spotlight's beam spilled out over the creases of Tom-Tom's neck and tailed away, glancing off the middle of his big back like a feather of moonlight; and here, its concentration and powers of reportage exhausted, the light did falsify. Like sea air itself, it removed all colour from the silk. Anna knew it was navy blue only because she had seen it earlier; and now it occurred to her that he had converted his costume not so much into a dressing gown as into the kind of large, clumsy clothes he wore for sailing; even the knee breeches and silk stockings, so elegantly designed to display the fine turning of a calf, had only to be peopled by his legs to take on the likeness of an old pair of trousers lumpily stuffed into the tops of gum boots. Where Anna had previously imagined a dressing gown cord holding him together she now supplied a length of old rope.

Tom-Tom did not ask his guests to sit down or to be silent. He no sooner stepped up on to the platform than the guests who had been standing on the dance floor, all uneasily turned towards the spotlight, decided to sit down. A patch here and there began it —as though blight had attacked a meadow: and then, with a soft, communal sighing, the whole body of people simply settled to the floor. Anna, peering into the dimness, could make out an impression as though the floor had been scattered with lumps of cushion.

Tom-Tom did not even hold up a hand. He stood on the platform; and chattering stopped. Finally, even the soft fidgeting on the floor stopped.

'He can always get silence,' Don Giovanni whispered to Anna. 'It's the same at board meetings.'

'He must have a presence,' Anna whispered back.

'It's not that. It's that money talks—and, when it does, the rest of us shut up.'

'It's all right, everyone,' Tom-Tom announced. 'You're not going to have to listen to me croon.'

The ballroom laughed.

'Where did he dig up that word?' Don Giovanni whispered. 'Nobody's *crooned* for twenty years.'

'You don't like him a bit, do you?' Anna murmured.

'I do, actually. It's just the proletarian in me. Guttersnipes are so called because they snipe. When I re-write *Midsummer Night's Dream*,' he added, close to her ear, 'the mechanicals are going to make sniping remarks while Theseus and Co. perform a classical tragedy.'

'. . . the next best thing', Tom-Tom was proclaiming, 'to

seeing the new year in in Paris, Mademoiselle Françoise Clouet. Soyez la bienvenue à Londres, Mademoiselle.' He stepped down out of the light.

'You're jealous of him,' Anna whispered. 'Perhaps *you*'re in love with Anne?'

'Hardly know her, actually,' said Don Giovanni; but he conceded Anna a wry look, sideways. 'It did cross my mind', he went on, 'whether you were an ex-mistress of Tom-Tom's. It seemed to account for your position in the house.'

'Hardly know him,' Anna replied; and conceded nothing.

A man without characteristics hurried on to the platform, shifted the double bass and sat rapidly down at the piano.

He was followed by a thin girl with thin straight colourless hair to her shoulders. She wore a short evening dress consisting of horizontal black frills which swaddled her tightly to just above the knees. Her legs, in very pale, peanut-coloured nylons, were thin, straight and apparently unbending—the legs of whitewood furniture: only the narrow knee cap made a small obstruction in the straightness, like an adam's apple; and when the girl took a step it looked as though her legs had swallowed. Her high-heeled shoes had a narrow, twenties-ish strap across the instep.

She paid no attention to her audience but stood with her back to them while she turned a nozzle of instructions on to her pianist, who sat with his head bent over the keyboard paying, in his turn, no attention to her.

At the outskirts of the ballroom a door opened, spilling a drop of light, and was rapidly and quietly closed. There followed the sound of whoever it had been tiptoeing about to find a place. In the moment of spilled light Anna pieced together that the edges of the ballroom had been filled up with chairs. They were the lightweight gilt-backed chairs which she had once, to tease Anne, called couturier's rococo. The ballroom was their usual place, but they had been cleared out for the dance; and now, Anna reconstructed, someone—probably Anne and the man-servant—had spent the past quarter of an hour unobtrusively sliding them back into the ballroom, as supplements to the rout benches which were already there, providing seats for the people who were too staid or too careful of their fancy dress to sit on the floor.

Suddenly the girl on the platform stopped talking to her accompanist and stepped into the centre of the spotlight.

A tenth of the audience clapped thinly and with embarrassment.

'I know just what we're in for,' Don Giovanni whispered to Anna. 'Three love songs and a ballad about Paris. One of the love songs—or possibly all three of the love songs—will say

<blockquote>
"Bonjour,
Amour."'
</blockquote>

The girl blew kisses into the audience, which became more embarrassed and provided a little more applause.

Her long, thin arms lingered at their fullest extent with each kiss, as if greedy to gather what applause there was. Finally she put both hands at once to her mouth and, with a heroic breaststroke, flung a double kiss. 'Merci. Merci.'

Edward, crunched up on the floor very close to Ruth's extended thigh, said:

'O Christ. Don't say it's all going to be in French.'

The pianist began to play a strummy accompaniment, contriving to make the piano sound like a ukulele.

By the very faint outermost illumination from the spot-light, falling just beyond the platform, Anna picked out Tom-Tom sitting on the floor. A slight upheaval brought a glitter of lamé into the light. Given the hint, Anna's eyes managed to trace the two broad shapes, reclining hip to hip, leaning one on the other: two old, long-married seals on a rock.

Françoise Clouet began to shout a love song.

Gently seated—rather like a balloon—on a gilt chair, near the door of the ballroom in case she should find it too hot and need to go out into the cooler air, Myra Blumen-baum leaned forward to Rudy, who was squatting on the floor at her feet, a little nervous about the sit of his kilt; she touched his shoulder.

He looked round anxiously. But she only wanted to smile at him—perhaps over the love song. He gave her a cheery little jerk with his head as he turned it back again.

'It reminds me——' Don Giovanni whispered; but a voice from the ballroom said, loudly:

'Shush.'

After a moment Anna took him by the silken wrist and made him tiptoe along to the recess at the end of the gallery. In slow motion she shook out a fold of the curtain, not daring to disturb the curtain rings, and wrapped them both up, leaving a declivity at the corner so that they could look out. Hardly breathing, she mouthed:

'*What* does it remind you of?'

'I've clean forgotten.'

She looked down into the ballroom but could no longer see Tom-Tom and Anne. Evidently they had slipped further into the darkness, seals sliding off the rock into the sea. Perhaps Anne had even left the ballroom altogether, going about some social business, rescuing guests shut out or seeing that the manservant got something to eat.

The applause for the love song was tremendous.

Françoise Clouet threw more kisses into the audience; and this time the kisses increased the audience's fervour. She had to hold up her hand to conjure a silence into which to say—her speaking voice not appreciably different from her singing voice:

'Et maintenant, une petite chanson——about Paris.'

The very announcement provoked applause.

The pianist cut it off by starting to play. It was the same accompaniment as for the previous song.

'I *know* it's going to rhyme Montmarte to Jean-Paul Sartre,' Don Giovanni whispered.

'. . . *ses parcs, ses cafés, ses trottoirs.*'

'. . . et ses pissoirs,' said Don Giovanni. 'Why doesn't she mention the principal tourist attraction?'

'Have you been to Paris?' Edward whispered to Ruth.
'Yes.'
A neighbour looked at their conversation unkindly. 'I went last summer,' Edward said. 'It wasn't nearly such hot stuff as I'd expected. But I think those places are really only meant for tourists.'
'Yes, we could hardly get *into* the Sainte Chapelle there were so many tourists,' Ruth replied. 'But then it isn't very big.'

During the louder than ever applause at the end, Don Giovanni said:
'O my mad student days on the Métro. The long bohemian search for Châtelet.'
The next song was of a different kind, though the accompaniment was the same as ever. This time the words were evidently more important: yet they were delivered

much more rapidly. After two lines Anna had to give up trying to understand. But from the ballroom there came a screech of self-admiring laughter every time the narrative turned the corner into another verse.

After the final verse, Anna said to Don Giovanni:

'It did contain my two words of argot, but as it contained a lot of others as well I couldn't follow it.'

'I followed it', he said, 'because I've heard it before. A French person played me the record of it and explained.'

'Well what does it say?'

'It's about a gorilla in the pay of the Russians who plays football for France and ends by scoring a de Gaulle. It's the sort of really hard-hitting, no-holds-barred political satire we just don't get in this country.' The next song everyone understood. It was the lament of a young woman whose rich husband was impotent. What no one understood was whether it was meant to be funny or sad. Françoise Clouet's delivery gave no hint, either way. The audience decided to shew no reaction during the song; but clapped roundly at the end.

Françoise Clouet began a straightforward love song. This time, instead of shouting, she muttered it, apparently in deference to the subject, as though love had been a bereavement.

'All this gooey love stuff,' Edward said. 'It gets monotonous. Let's go and sit in your father's car for a bit.'

'Don't be silly,' Ruth said. 'We'd freeze.'

Anna sensed that Don Giovanni's satirical impulse was spent. In herself she had ceased to feel any impulses at all. Not by design, merely by an exhausted gravitation, they let themselves be drawn back into recess, until they were both leaning against the rear wall of the gallery.

Anna had propped the curtain in such a way as to leave them a peephole, but from where she stood she could not see out of it.

Presently the curtain slid a little under its own weight. It paused: for a minute; for a minute and a half: and then, when she had stopped expecting it, it gave a weighty swoosh and dropped sheer to the floor of the gallery.

The peephole was quite cut off. But she was too tired to step forward and make it again.

Only an infinitesimal amount of light reached them: accidental fragments of the spotlight or perhaps reflexions from it, seeping round the curtain. The curtain muffled the love song, too; such tune as it had was almost too blurred for them to pick it out as a tune. They were surrounded by the smell of dust.

Edward whispered:
'It's got a heater, hasn't it?'
'You have to switch the engine on.'
'Well what about rugs? Aren't there some rugs?'

'Actually,' said Don Giovanni, as though it took an effort for him to speak, 'I like Siamese cats rather better than the ordinary kind.'

'I like you,' Anna said, without any emphasis or expression at all.

'I bet your mother never stirs out without being *swathed* in rugs.'

Don Giovanni made no reply to what she had said. But after a little she discerned that he was peering through the dimness towards her, towards the place at the rise of her breasts where, a little more to the left than to the right, she had stuck a beauty spot.

'I like your beauty spot,' he said. 'I've liked it all night.'

'I like you,' she repeated, in the same way as before.

'Yet the curious thing is', he said, 'that although I like it I want to take it off.'

'O all right,' Ruth said. 'I can do my diary there. It's going to be rather difficult writing down all the French.'

Anna said:

'That's one of the things I'd prefer to do for myself.'

'All right. Then do.'

She looked down at her bosom, which in the dimness

was a greenish white, the colour of flesh in an old painting on panel.

She put her thumbnail under the edge of the beauty spot. Slowly she peeled it off, held out her hand and let the beauty spot tumble invisibly to the floor.

'You realise', he said, 'that you've made me terrified to touch you?'

'Yes. I've been enjoying your terror for some minutes.'

'Are you cruel?' he asked.

She seemed to be breathless for a moment. 'My cruelty is very, very delicate,' she eventually replied. slowly.

'That's as though you were going to behead me and promised that no single stroke would be fatal: you'd just do it with hundreds of little ones.'

His voice sounded to her extraordinarily loud and deep, but it could not have penetrated the muffling of the curtain because no one from the ballroom called Shush.

'I'd rather thought it was you who were going to execute me,' she said, with a quiver, possibly a laugh, in the sentence. 'You wear the executioner's mask.'

'Perhaps both. Each each.'

She said and did nothing.

His head bent forward, towards her, as though for the executioner's stroke, and he began very passionately to kiss the place where the beauty spot had been.

9

'O God,' Anna said, pulled almost off balance by his embrace and also shaken by the violence of her desire to embrace him.

'Is it all right?' he said quickly, anxiously, through the darkness. 'What's the matter?'

'Nothing,' she said promptly. 'It's all right. It's just that I didn't know I felt so—violently about it. Isn't it awful', she went on, 'to be surprised by one's own feelings, at my age. And my feelings go veering about.' She put up her hand and stroked the side of his face, encountering the mask and taking care not to disturb it. 'But I won't be a bitch this time. I really won't.'

'That's just as well,' he said. 'Because this time . . .'

'Yes, I know . . . No, if I hesitate now, it's purely because of practical considerations.'

'Yes, well, obviously, not *here*,' he said, casting a look round the gallery—more for illustration than in the hope of seeing much through the gloom. 'Come to my flat.'

'That's not the only practical consideration.'

'O,' he said impatiently, 'I've got plenty.'

'I don't know', she said, consideringly, 'that we shall

need *plenty* . . .'

The mask stopped responding to the fluctuations of his expression and remained stretched taut and stiff for a full moment, while he was shocked. Then he realised she had consented and she felt the mask crease—fold and collapse inwards—as he gave a great grin.

'Come to my flat,' he repeated. 'We'll probably pick up a taxi. Anyway, it's only a mile or two. It's in—'

She put her hand across his mouth.

He kissed and then gently bit at her fingers.

'Be careful,' she said. 'Be anonymous.'

His hand removed her hand from his mouth.

'Let me just say—' he began, but instead of saying anything his mouth made its way violently into hers. Her hand placed his hand on her breast, and it violently grasped her.

'O God,' Anna said again.

This time he made no comment, accepting it.

'I'm just shameless,' she said. 'I just want to take you to the nearest bed.'

'Well, come there,' he answered.

He softly tugged open the door at the back of the gallery. Even the dim lighting from the corridor outside was enough to bite at her eyes. She shut them for a moment and groped her way through; felt for the banister and then for the three shallow steps leading down from the gallery. She heard him quietly shut the door behind them, almost wholly sealing off the French love song in the ballroom.

She opened her eyes and walked along the corridor.

He came hurrying after her, caught her up, and put his hand beneath her elbow. 'Get your coat.'

'No, listen,' she said, halting suddenly, so that he almost tumbled over her. Instead of retreating he remained huddled close against her. She turned towards him, and he was so close that she had to draw her head backwards before she could search for his eyes through the slits of his mask. 'Listen,' she said. 'I *am* an iconoclast.'

'I know you are . . .'

'Do you believe', she asked, her voice betraying that she was almost suffocated by the excitement of her own mischief, even while she tried to phrase the idea as formally as possible in order to calm, or to arrange, the excitement, 'that perfect bad taste is almost as hard to achieve as perfect good taste?'

'Well I don't know,' he said in a delaying voice, not so much in reluctance against her plan as in fear that it might involve a change in his. 'I don't know what you're . . .'

She slipped her fingers round his wrist, just as she had when she made him tiptoe along the gallery. But this time she moved much more swiftly and easily. She reversed their direction. She led him back along the corridor; past the entrance to the gallery; along to the far end of the corridor: to the second staircase.

He came perfectly obediently and passively, just as he

126

had tiptoeing along the gallery: but this time his hand was active. His wrist twisted and slithered inside her grip as though her grip was a handcuff, and his fingers flapped and bent upwards, trying to make contact with her hand and insinuate themselves into it.

She started up the stairs, drawing him, willing, behind her. With determination, she did not look back at him.

She made him almost run up the first flight.

He offered no protest.

The next flight she had to take more slowly herself.

Halfway up, she said, but still without looking back:

'This was originally the servants' staircase. It seems appropriate to our position in this house.'

He gave no answer, or only a 'Mm'.

Speaking had made her out of breath. In her own deeper breathing she could not hear whether he was out of breath, too.

The staircase was badly lit, by only an occasional bulb on the landings. The whole house seemed empty and quiet. There was only the noise of their footsteps, the plain wood creaking beneath them, Anna's breathing and from time to time a squelch, a sound almost of sap being bruised, when the high heels of Anna's shoes actually dug into the naked surface of the wood.

Against her desire, Anna found that the higher she mounted, and the higher her excitement and hurry, the slower she had to go.

A few steps from the top, she paused altogether, altogether out of breath. She took the opportunity to slip off her shoes, which were making too much noise. Don Giovanni steadied her while she took them off; but she still would not look round at him.

Splinters in the surface of the wooden tread pulled at threads in the sole of her stockings.

She put her two shoes together and held them in one hand. Her other hand groped behind her, to resume Don Giovanni's wrist. He thrust it at her.

She ran up the last few steps, and he followed her to the door of Anne's bedroom.

Softly Anna opened the door. She groped round the jamb, found the light switch and put it on, knowing that the sudden brightness might affront their eyes but wanting Don Giovanni to see the room instantly and whole.

Her eyes *were* affronted. For a moment she could not understand the heavings, the upheaval, in the oval white bed. She had illuminated the back of a neck, ochre coloured; with difficulty she recognised that she had lately been looking at it illuminated by a spotlight; but now its voice was spluttering and its huge body was straining in an effort to roll over sideways, to roll *off*, like a seal trying to roll off a rock; and, as it did manage to heave a little up and roll a little to one side, it revealed another head on the pillow, face up, a startled face, the face of its wife, the face which had been *beneath* . . .

Anna brushed the light out, jammed the door shut, snatched with her free hand at Don Giovanni and ran back to the top of the stairs and then down the first flight.

From behind the closed door above her she faintly heard the frightened, creaking 'Caw caw caw' of the kitten.

Don Giovanni followed her.

She tumbled her way down the next flight, not caring whether she missed a step, took two steps at a time, bumped the newel of the banisters in hurling herself round . . .

She stopped, and the noise of her hurry stopped, perhaps two thirds of the way down, only because she had let one of her shoes tumble out of her hand. It somersaulted to a couple of steps below where she had stopped, and rested there. She lacked the energy for the precise movements of going the further two steps, bending down and retrieving it.

Don Giovanni came down the stairs behind her. He hesitated; passed her; descended and picked up the shoe. He handed it back, and she took it.

He mounted a step.

He stood face to face with her, one step below her.

'O my dear, how *grotesque*,' she said.

She bent her head towards his chest and burst into tears there.

10

'You see,' Anna said. 'I just can't be perfect.'

They sat down side by side on the stairs. No one came. The house was still silent.

'I over-reached myself,' she said. 'I thought I could carry off something that was beyond me.'

She looked down at his handkerchief between her hands. She had been surprised to see the ordinary twentieth-century handkerchief coming out of his eighteenth-century pocket. She gave it back to him. He stretched his silken leg out, down the steps, in order to get the handkerchief to the mouth of his pocket.

'I've made the front of your costume damp,' Anna said, glancing at it.

He gave a deprecating move of the head.

'She has a perfect right,' Anna said. 'Her own husband.' She added: 'Her own house. Her own party.'

'Yes.'

'How *can* I feel betrayed?'

'One's feelings aren't always logical.'

'It's *her* bed.'

She put her forefinger on the pouch of flesh just below

her eye. She did not want to rub the eye, for fear of blurring the mascara; so she depressed the flesh into a waterspout, a gargoyle, through which to channel off the remaining tears, which were already cool.

'It may be rather comic,' she said. 'Though it *is* grotesque as well. Especially if you knew what he calls her in bed.' Then: 'Have I ruined my mascara?'

He twisted to face her and scrutinised the underneath of her eyes.

'It's run a bit,' he said.

He stretched his leg out again, got at the handkerchief again and offered it to her.

She made it into a fingerstall, licked the tip, touched it to her eyes and said:

'Guide me.'

He did so.

'That's all we can do about it,' she said, stopping his finger; and he put his handkerchief away again. 'You'll have to take me as I am. I've left my make-up case up there.'

'Up there?'

'Up there,' she said wryly. 'On the dressing table, I think. Or the bed.'

'I hope they moved it,' he said.

'I'm sorry you didn't see the kitten.'

'I heard it, I think.'

'I hope they moved that.'

'You're very tired,' he said. 'Come to my flat. You needn't be seduced.'

'I want to be.'

But neither of them moved from the stairs.

'I expect you're too tired,' Anna said. 'I've made you run up and down the stairs. For nothing. The servants' stairs are always more steep, because nobody cared about *them*.'

'Get your coat.'

This time they did stand up.

11

She found him waiting for her, his back turned to where she must appear from, in the hall. No one else was there.

He had put on an ordinary black topcoat over his costume, and the fact that no trousers emerged from beneath its hem was farcical.

'My dear,' she said going up behind him, 'you look like a bishop.'

'You're giving a perfectly respectable adventure an air of scandal,' he replied.

In his coat he looked larger—which put it in Anna's mind to take his arm, cling to it, and chatter to him.

The sedan chair which she had seen carried bodily into the ballroom now stood empty, unlit, in a corner of the hall, a large egg that had hatched.

'Perhaps it'll be snowing,' Anna said.

'Wouldn't that be perfect?'

He opened the front door for her.

'No,' she said. 'It isn't snowing.'

As he stepped through the shallow portico of the house, his hand went up to his face and he tilted his head, beginning to slip it out of the mask.

'Stop,' Anna said.

He stopped: both what he was doing, and walking. 'Don't be absurd,' he said. 'I can't walk through the street in a mask.'

'If you take it off, I'm not coming.'

'That's sheerest blackmail. I can't stop a cab with a mask on. The man'll think it's a hold-up.'

'I'll stop the cab.'

'O don't—'

'Then he'll only think you're drunk. You can tell him where to go through the partition.'

'The whole business is quite absurd,' he said, taking her arm and propelling her forward, but protestingly. 'Do you realise I don't even know what to call you?'

'You can call me Anna. I'll allow you to drop the Donna.'

'Of course Anna might be your real name.'

'It might.'

There was nothing to shew it ever had snowed except a particularly glittering, anvil-hard patch at the centre of each paving stone, which might indicate that a few flakes had settled, melted and then frozen again.

Certainly the air was freezing. That was apparent from the clear frosty look of the light from the street lamps, which seemed suspended like icy lemons in the bare branches of the trees that lined the pavement. Cars were parked thickly, along the whole cul-de-sac, up the slight, slightly twisted, asphalted hill by which the cul-de-sac turned into the main road. Under the street lamps the car tops gleamed with frost.

'I'm not so inquisitive,' Anna said. 'For all I know, it was your wife who arrived at the ball in a sedan chair. Her name might even be Elvira.'

'I guarantee', he said, with an appearance of cunning, 'that no wife of mine is at that ball.'

'No, I didn't think you'd ever been married,' Anna said.

'I'm not very good at this game, am I?'

'You're improving.'

'I don't think my heart's in it. I wish I knew about your husband.'

'He's alive and well. I heard from him for Christmas.'

'Then you don't live with him?'

'Perhaps I've been a little unfair,' Anna said. 'I promise you, he's not even in this country.'

He looked down at her: gratified. 'And do you suppose', he asked, happily resuming the game, 'that my name is Giovanni?'

'It seems unlikely.'

'John, then?'

'Sheer statistics would favour that in any case.'

'Had you considered', he cunningly put it, 'that it might be Donald?'

She did consider it. 'No,' she said at last, 'I don't think you're Scottish. Even though your present appearance might mislead people into supposing that you're wearing a kilt.'

She noticed as they passed that the dark green door of one of the cars parked on the little hill, near the top of the cul-de-sac, bore, painted on it, like fake armorial bearings, the little rebus—a tree in blossom— whereby Rudy was accustomed, on his writing paper, his book plate, his table napkin rings, to pun on the name Blumenbaum.

Edward had protested against leaving the light on, saying it hurt his eyes. But Ruth said that to write up her diary by the light of the street lamp alone might hurt her eyes permanently.

She started the entry on a fresh page, so that Edward could not read what had gone before.

Watching over her shoulder, he said:

'It wasn't about a gorilla.'

'It was. Didn't you hear her keep singing "Un gorille"?'

'It can't have been. Or the word must have some slang meaning. I was sure it was about politics.'

When he heard voices and footsteps approach, he flicked off the light switch and pulled Ruth down to kneel on the floor of the car.

'What are you *doing?*'

'Someone's coming.'

'Well what does it matter? We aren't stealing anything.'

'Keep your head down.'

Nonetheless Ruth raised it enough to look through the window.

'It's Anna,' she said. 'She's going home with that man.'

Edward tumbled over to Ruth's side of the car, in time to watch the two figures walking away, up the hill, into the main road.

'I *thought* she must be quite experienced,' he said. 'Unless he's her husband?'

'No. She's divorced,' Ruth said.

She sat up on the seat again, re-arranged the rug over her lap and resumed her diary. She did not bother to put on the light again. The street lamp did give enough illumination for her to write, in large capitals:

'*ANNA K. IS A WHORE.*'

'Can't you see?' Don Giovanni whispered to Anna in the cab. 'He *is* worried about the mask.'

'Then set his mind at rest.'

'How?'

'Kiss me.'

'Let's just snuggle under the rug and be cosy for a bit,' Edward said, sliding far down on the seat.

To Ruth his remark seemed so uncharacteristic of him that she felt on guard. It was even uncharacteristic of him not to want the light on. He was not a person who preferred half-dark.

Now that he was suddenly unaggressive she paradoxically felt more strained in relation to him. She sat rather stiff and high up against the back of the car, riding the rear seat like an old-fashioned bicycle, trying to resist the insinuating downward tendency of his warm snuggly body beneath the rug.

Her eyes rested on the light switch, as though she was putting it on by thought. It was high on the side wall, between the ·doors, at the dividing point between the front and the back of the car. It was well in front of her, rather to her left and, in the high, rigid car, quite out of her reach. But by fixing her eyes on it she seemed to anchor her body against being drawn deeper into the soft slippery nest Edward was making of the back of the car.

Her mind was really on something else; but her thoughts seemed to be enquiring why the light switches in cars could not be of the ordinary pattern but consisted of a little square-sided stick of brownish plastic, and what motoring purpose it could serve to make the end of the stick grooved, like the milling— but wider—on coins.

Don Giovanni poured a handful of silver into her hand so that she could pay the driver while he opened the front door of the block of flats.

The driver must have turned round during the journey and seen them occupied in kissing: even so Anna thought him relieved to be quit of them. His relief bounced like a spring in his voice as he called, loudly so that it would reach the man standing on the steps:

'Happy new year!'

They replied perfunctorily, Anna embarrassed because the driver must take them for husband and wife returning home, Don Giovanni bodily embarrassed because he did not want to turn round on the steps and let the mask be seen again.

She ran across the pavement and up the steps to join him as hurriedly as if it *had* been snowing: it was cold enough to: and with her hands she made blinkers for her eyes, as though to keep out a blizzard,

'I didn't see anything,' she said as he pushed open the front door for her. 'I have no idea whatever where we are.'

He punched the three-minute switch in the hall. 'Second floor.' They began to walk up the marble stairs.

'Didn't you hear when I gave the driver the address?'

'I put my hands over my ears.'

'Of course, if you once heard the number, you'd never forget.'

'Are my shoes making too much noise?'

'No, you needn't take them off this time. People expect a certain amount of noise on new year's eve.'

'New year's day.'

'Yes, new year's day.'

He unlocked the front door of his flat.

The hall inside was a mere carpeted cupboard. It revealed nothing about him. It hadn't space to.

He pushed open a door. 'Come in here.' His hand

reached in front of her and pushed down a light switch, but no light came on. 'O, it needs to be put on beside the bed. It's one of those two-way arrangements. I always catch it on the wrong foot.'

'Don't put it on,' she said.

He stopped, having groped half way across the room.

'You're absurd,' he said.

She shut the bedroom door behind them.

'You're making a fetish of anonymity. I take it it's that? You don't want to see where I live? Anyway, your purpose is defeated before you start. The light from the hall shews under the door. There's a house light on the front of the block just outside my window, and it doesn't go out all night. And I'm going to switch on the electric fire, which gives a little light.'

The fire stood in a disused hearth. He switched it on, and it began to hum.

'All right,' she said. 'Then there's enough light. We don't need any more.'

'You must be able to see quite clearly.'

'It must all look different, though, in this light. Not like itself. Of course it looks the same to you, because you know it.'

She looked round. His bed was a single bed. She picked her way over to the hearth.

'It takes a minute or two for it to warm up the place,' he said, his head alluding down to the electric fire, 'And to stop humming.' He went on, in a friendlier voice: 'What note's it humming on?'

'The A below middle C.'

She picked up an invitation card that was propped on his mantelpiece, carried it a step or two—it was a small room—to the window, folded the top of the card out of sight in case his name had been written there and read the rest in the light from outside. It was the invitation to the ball.

'Eighteenth-century costume
10 p.m.—dawn',

it said at the bottom right-hand corner.

'I must leave before dawn,' Anna said, putting the folded card back on the shelf, 'or I *shall* see your room, against my will.'

The fire stopped humming.

'A for Anna,' he said, 'of course?'

'Of course.'

He approached behind her and laid his hands on the lapels of her coat. 'Are you warm enough?'

She slipped out of her coat and he put it carefully over a chair.

He came back, approached in the same way and from behind her laid his hands on the straps of her dress.

'O, that's more baffling,' she said. 'Many a waiter has been frustrated by that.' She began to unfasten it. 'Undress quickly,' she bade him. 'It's cold.'

He took off his coat and then began to peel off his silk costume, letting the pieces slide to the floor. It all came quite easily and logically to pieces—he was Harlequin disassembled, the lozenges shuffled in the kaleidoscope—although when it was all on him you could not see where the joins would come.

Naked, Anna scurried into his bed, exaggerating the chill which made her shiver and huddle down, because she felt a little shy.

The electric fire threw a crimson wash over his bare skin.

12

'Wait,' Anna said, letting her hand, which had been stroking the side of his face, pause on the mask. 'It's absurd you should be wearing this.'

He tried to prop himself on one elbow and get his other hand up to hold some point on the mask while he twisted his head out of it.

'Let me do it,' she said. 'Indeed, I think I owe it to you.'

He dropped his head forward on to her breast and she, craning up a little so she could see her fingers working at the back of his head, unfastened the black tapes.

He eased his face sideways to help her peel off the mask, which she dropped over the side of the bed.

His forehead descended on her breast again.

She clasped her two hands to the sides of his head and pressed it between her palms, almost convulsively and yet carefully, as though his head had been an easter egg.

A groove ran round the back of his head, a declivity in the hair left by the tapes, like the brand left on someone who had been wearing an eye patch.

'No,' she whispered, lifting his head a little between her hands. 'Let me *see* you.'

He raised himself.

She looked at his face, making it out quite well by the light from outside the window. It was simply a man's face. The two halves, the one she knew and the one she had never seen, fitted together logically, and into a quite comely whole. The eyes were more handsome than they had appeared through the slits; and surrounded by a new context, they looked strange to her. Perhaps in fancy, perhaps by an illusion of the unsatisfactory light, the part of the face which had been covered seemed to shew signs of it: nothing so pronounced as the shoot-pallid look of skin that had emerged from sticking plaster; more like the imprecisely naked look of eyes that normally wore spectacles when the spectacles were removed.

'Is it all right?' he asked, almost unhappily.

'It's marvellous.'

'O, it's not that, I'm afraid.'

'No . . .' she agreed. 'But if it's not beautiful it seems to me very ornamental.'

He acknowledged the remark, with a touch of a smile.

'Really, you know,' Anna said, 'I've met men's faces for the first time from many strange angles and in many strange situations but never, before, in *this* situation. . .'

She saw on his face that moment's rigidity, the rigidity of being shocked, which previously she had perceived only transmitted through the velvet of the mask.

He gave, his face still rigid, the first wing, a mere flutter, which he left uncompleted, of a laugh.

The flutter was transmuted into a flutter inside her body. The rigidity of his look dissolved.

Then his head plunged, and his face was lost to her. She lost the wish to see it, the memory even that it existed, in the response of her sensations to his labouring body: until she suddenly emerged, at the end of the same are of sensations which had begun with the flutter of his laugh and of his body, to the knowledge that her sensations had passed the point up to which she was free to go back on them, and that she was now free to have thoughts again, since her voyage to pleasure was from now on involuntary.

Having only to wait, she—or some part of her, perhaps her hand on his head, perhaps her mouth on his shoulder—convulsively, repetitively and in the end, she felt, abrasively, caressed his body; it was done with the mere idleness of excited yet reluctant impatience, a musician sawing at the unending rhythms of Bach; as though by digging into his flesh, by pitting him, her fingers or teeth could actually lay hold on the paradox whereby so much thought and strategy in the vertical world went towards manoeuvring into this horizontal situation where pleasure consisted in something being imposed, in being carried beyond the point of no return, in suffering an act as unwilled as sneezing, falling asleep or dying. Suffering, sobbing, swelling, sawing, sweating, her body was at last convulsed by the wave that broke inside it: and the image which was dashed up on to the walls of her mind and deposited like droplets there, distinct but quite passive, was of the rococo cartouche which broke everlastingly over the walls of Anne's bedroom, perpetually but without moisture drenching the white satin with drops like drops of glycerine or sweat.

Anna lay listening bodily to her after-sensations. An intense, deep-buried throbbing shook the lower part of her body as sobbing might have shaken the upper. Indeed, these throbs seemed to her an exact counterpart and antonym to sobs. They made an outburst, a shower, of pleasure: the opposite of a storm of weeping. In a storm of weeping there would have been, as in all storms, a wry warmth and happiness, if only for the relief and release: and equally, in this most intense, least voluntary and therefore most death-imaging of pleasures there was—and also for the release—a wry sadness.

PART THREE

13

Tom-Tom made a great fuss about the fact that they had been intruded upon. All the time he was dressing, stuffing himself back into his costume, whose navy blue surface was now completely crumpled into facets like the surface of a sea, he complained and speculated about who, and how, it could have been.

Anne was concerned only to make him hurry. She told him that the cabaret, which had been their opportunity, must be long finished; that guests must be seeking hosts; that some guests probably wanted to take their leave; that if he did not come soon *hundreds* of them would invade upstairs.

Tom-Tom talked himself into the explanation that it had been a guest who did not know the house and was searching for the lavatory.

Anne did not contradict him. Yet she was fairly sure that she had—and she had, after all, had the advantage of being face up—recognised Anna in the lighted doorway. She reconstructed that Anna had come to reclaim her make-up case. Anne, who knew it was there—who had, in fact, lifted it down on to the floor—blamed herself for not taking thought and locking the door.

She blamed herself more incisively for, now, not saying any of this to Tom-Tom. She scrupulously liked to report to him everything that passed in her mind. But she could not bring herself to risk antagonising him against Anna when she was not even sure it had been Anna. She decided to wait and, some time, some time when she could find her, ask Anna. Then, if it had been, she would tell Tom-Tom: and by then the lapse of time would have made him less apt to be antagonised.

He had never shewn himself in the least jealous of Anna. Yet Anne, for fear he should be, often played down her affection for her friend when she spoke to Tom-Tom: but from time to time, when she caught herself in this habit of playing down, her scrupulousness obliged her to correct for it, and she would make to Tom-Tom a formal declaration of her affection for Anna.

All that worried her now about the intrusion—all, indeed, that even held it in her memory—was the thought that she might know the true explanation and be concealing it from Tom-Tom. The incident itself, from the moment the actual fright had passed, seemed to her a nothing. She bundled it away as the sort of thing that always happened to one in foreign hotels: it had surely happened to her, she imprecisely remembered, on all four of her honeymoons.

All the street lamps had gone out.

*

Ruth felt justified in leaning forward and switching on the light, whatever protest it might bring from Edward.

However, although his body jerked when Ruth disturbed him by heaving forward, and again when the light went on, he did not wake up. After a moment his head turned away from the light, and away from Ruth, his profile disintegrating, his mouth opening against the back of the seat. Still without waking up, he began to gulp, chokingly.

Rather frightened, Ruth thought of waking him up. She remembered that during her first year at school a girl in her dormitory had made even more frightening sounds— sounds of strangulation—in her sleep, and yet had never come to any harm. After a minute Edward stopped gulping.

Ruth took out her diary and pencil. Under the entry 'ANNA K. IS A WHORE,' she wrote:

'Supose I am, too, now (3.22 a.m.)'

Presently, the light still on inside the car, she fell asleep again. Her head slipped down towards the side window, at the opposite extreme from Edward's, although their bodies remained in warm dishevelled contact beneath the rug. The two together made a shape as though, at the back of the silent, lighted interior, an enormous flower had opened to its fullest, its almost overblown, extent.

Anna's eyes opened and disclosed to her that she was lying not merely face down but face half over the edge of the bed, looking down at the floor boards.

On one of the floor boards lay a piece of paper.

She let her hand trail over the floor, which was slightly dusty, and pick up the paper·

She recognised that it must have slid out of Don Giovanni's pocket when he undressed·

The poor light would not have permitted her to read it if she had not known in advance what it said:

'. . . *what is true is that she is one of the hero's victims*. . .'

3.50 a.m.Wd. like to cross out previous entries but vowed no alterations. All the same, feel this diary should take more dispassionate tone: facts, not feelings. Went to sleep after having sex with Ed. in back of car. Thought it nasty, short and brutish. Have just noticed it is snowing.

'What are you doing?'

'I was trying not to wake you,' Anna said

'But what are you doing?' He had neither moved nor opened his eyes.

'I think it must be dawn.'

'It can't be.'

'"It was the nightingale and not the lark". O my dear, it *can* be, though I don't know if it is.'

'My watch is on the mantelpiece.'

'It looked lighter, all of a sudden.'

'What does my watch say?'

From the window she told him:

'It's not dawn. It's snow.'

'Snow? Then it *is* perfect.' He went to sleep again.

She began to get dressed.

After a little, he said:

'Why are you getting dressed?'

'I'm going back to the party.'

'Not yet.'

'I haven't said goodbye to Anne.'

'Neither have I.'

'I'll say it for you.'

'No, I'm coming.' Again, he fell asleep.

While she pinned the black lace to her hair again, she watched the snowflakes tumbling past the window and thought that his consciousness must equally be drifting and spinning down into the dark.

He got out of bed. 'You can't say goodbye for me. You don't know who I am.'

Dressed, he picked up the mask and dangled it. 'I don't have to put this on again?'

'For those who understand symbolism it will be instructive to have seen you arrive in it and then come back without it.'

'You yourself', he said, 'have lost your beauty spot.'

14

As soon as she saw that the snow was lying, Ruth Blumenbaum wanted to get out of the car and into the snow. She visually imagined the flakes drifting about her figure, their whiteness merging into the white of her costume: herself freezing in a statue's pose, as though in the game of statues: herself petrified, *become* a statue, a garden statue, with a furrow of snow piling up like a fur tippet along her arms: herself a snow-man, a Cherubino of snow, a snow page. At the same time the nerves in her skin were also imagining. They prefigured the icy burning touch of the snow, which would purify her.

Yet for some reason she did not want to get out of the car alone. So she woke Edward.

Her first attempt only set him gulping. She had to thump his shoulder with her fist—though as a matter of fact she did not want to touch him. But the instant she told him that there was snow and that it was lying he came to consciousness willingly, even eagerly.

Although she had herself thought of the snow as a purification, she was offended by the welcoming way he went hopping out of the car into it. Although she had hated the intimate contact of their bodies in the car she felt that in shaking it off with such obvious pleasure he was betraying it, like a man betraying hearth and home.

She switched off the light and followed him resentfully out of the car.

'My God, this is just what we needed,' he said. He stood for a moment, shoulders scrunched up, hands in his coat pockets flat against his hips, white flakes tumbling about his black figure. Then:

'Come on,' he said, vigorously.

'Come on what?'

'Make a snow man, of course.'

'It seems a pity to spoil it,' she said, looking round. 'It's so beautiful.'

He stooped and began working.

Yet when she looked at it, although it was beautiful, she was not sure that she liked it. It was not reassuring. The road in which she had gone to sleep had been changed while she slept.

Also, although it looked as soft and warm as a woolly animal, the actual touch of the snow was much more stingingly, even numbingly, cold than her nerves had been able to imagine.

She went and fetched the rug from the car, and draped it round her shoulders.

'Do something,' Edward said, looking up and observing her. 'That's the way to keep warm.'

She stooped and began scraping together a little hump of snow, in which her fingers left grooves.

'Not like that,' Edward said. 'It won't even stand up if you make it like that. Won't be firm enough.'

But she went on for a moment or two in the same way. While she bent, the edges of the rug dripped loose over her arms, sometimes getting in her way, sometimes threatening that the whole rug was going to slip off.

Presently she stopped working and leaned against the side of the car, watching Edward work.

'There's more to making a snow man than you'd think. It's'—he was panting—'a highly skilled job.'

Ruth tried to observe him as a person: but she could see in him only a representative of his sex.

'You start with a snowball. And then you just have to get down and roll it, and roll it, and roll it, until it gets bigger, and bigger . . .'

'What for?' she asked, unthinking.

'The body, of course.' He rolled it through the snow on the ground. Already it was the size of a baby.

To Ruth's eye, every gesture he made, every pore of his body, was stamped with the fact:— masculine. His very sentences, let alone his sentiments, his very words, even, seemed distinguished from words a woman might say. She believed that the least sexual part of the human body—that a little toenail—that a clipping from a little toenail—must betray, must be impregnated with, the sex of its owner.

While he worked, the snow stopped falling.

Between men and women she felt an unbridgeable divorce: she was convinced that two minds of different sex could never achieve identity of content.

He carried his large, roly-poly snowball on to the pavement, where he planted it down alongside the car.

It looked like a stump, a column cut off.

He squared it off a bit at the top, with his hands. Then he squatted beside it and heaped up a little snow skirt, pleated by his fingers, all the way round the base, to make sure it would stand steady.

'Now the head.'

He stooped for a handful of snow and stood compacting it this way and that between his hands.

'There's the beginning. Fortunately, this one needn't be so big.'

He bent down and began to roll his snowball, like a marble, up the slope, in the gutter.

'Someone's coming,' Ruth said.

He snatched up his snowball in one hand and Ruth's wrist in the other and made her run out into the road and then duck down, on the far side, behind the car.

'It's Anna,' Ruth whispered. 'With that man.'

Their steps made only a crunch in the snow: but their voices and laughter were clear.

'He's taken off his mask,' Edward whispered.

'Where are they going?'

'Back to the house, back to the ball. This road doesn't lead anywhere else.'

Ruth peered out again. She saw Anna's head evidently alluding to the snow man as they walked past it, and heard her voice say:

'The man of stone. The statue *has* come to your supper party.'

'He lacks a head,' the man answered.

'Nodded too hard in the graveyard scene,' said Anna's voice, walking out of earshot.

'I like her cheek,' Edward whispered, exhaling both in admiration and in relaxation because the two figures had passed. 'Fancy daring to come *back*.'

Ruth looked swiftly down at his hand.

'Throw it,' she said.

'What? This?'

'Be quick.'

He stepped out on to the pavement. He stood poised at the top of the little hill.

Already the two figures were nearly at the house. Light from its windows reached out to them, snaring them in a frosty net, in which they were held up clear to Edward's aim.

He threw his snowball; and then threw himself back into hiding, slithering on his knees in the snow, next to Ruth.

'Did you hit her?'

'Slap in the middle of the back. No, higher. Between the shoulder blades.'

But neither of them felt any laughter to stifle.

Ruth looked out.

The couple was still standing at the foot of the hill, at the entrance to the house. The two figures were vividly black. The man was still looking round, angrily or at least enquiringly; the woman holding his arm and making gestures of belittling the hurt or, perhaps, of dissuading him from pursuing enquiry or vengeance.

At last, the man put his arm round the woman and drew her towards the house.

There was still a trace of snow, which he had not managed to brush off, on the back of her coat.

Light from the house caught and splintered on the sequins attached to the lace the woman wore at the back of her hair. Perhaps through something she had read, but more probably through cinema stills she had seen, Ruth was reminded of snowy platforms, of Russia, of—she had at last to admit—Anna Karenina. The woman's head was wholly veiled in frosty air, as though someone had breathed round it and the breath had remained, opaque, on the still, cold atmosphere of the night, like white scratches engraved on a black sheet of ice.

15

Anne looked into the ballroom, saw Anna was not there and decided to—if only her guests would remain *settled* long enough—look for her upstairs. As she felt the approach of dawn and still had not found Anna, she became more and more remorseful towards her. She knew of nothing to justify the remorse except the tiny betrayal of having abandoned Anna to Dr. Brompius; that, and the fact, which was not her fault, that she had *not* found Don Giovanni for Anna. Yet in the absence of Anna—which might be a symptom itself; Anne could imagine her using her knowledge of the house to seek out a corner to weep in—Anne felt herself cut off from the supply of her friend's thoughts. Not only did she not know what Anna was thinking: Anna did not know what *she* was thinking: Anna might, it seemed to her, spin out of her ignorance some far more monstrous betrayal than had ever been intended and attribute it, so wrongly, to Anne.

Since she had taken them off and put them on again without washing them in between, Anne's stockings sat loosely on her legs. Stretched once to the shape of the elephantine knees, they could not adapt themselves to the same knees now occupying them from a slightly different point of entry. As she went up the grand staircase Anne tugged surreptitiously at one of her suspenders through the lamé, hoping to induce it to hold the stocking more taut. But it would not. And as a matter of fact the lamé, too, was sitting loosely, for the same reason; she could hardly have washed that, but she might, if she had taken thought in time, have hung it up, or at least stretched it properly over something, just as she might have locked the bedroom door. It seemed to be with a shrug of self-reproach that her lamé covering—her pachydermous lamé covering—moved loosely over the great folding undulations of her body. She planted her footsteps wearily up the staircase: a very old working elephant going about its work.

Don Giovanni stretched Anna's coat over the cabin of the sedan chair in the hall, to give it a chance to dry.

Seeing it stretched there, with a patch of moisture at the centre of the centre panel of the fabric, Anna re-experienced the sensation of receiving the snowball on her back. She also remembered, more faintly, the feeling she had had, when she and Rudy had been cut in on, of sensing the knuckles which tapped him in the nerves of her own back: her senses had appropriated the intruder's summons, acknowledging that it was a summons for her—and yet it had turned out to have nothing to do with her, since the knocking on the back had come from Ruth Blumenbaum's beau.

Don Giovanni, seeing her looking at the place where the snowball had hit the coat, said what he had already said outside, before leading her into the house:

'It must have been just a stray snowball. I'm sure no one was trying to hit you.'

This time he revealed also why he insisted on that construction of it, by adding:

'You mustn't feel there's anyone who's hostile to you.'

'I don't,' she said. 'It's all right. I don't feel aimed at.'

Satisfied, he took off his own coat and threw it over one of the handles of the sedan chair; they had been left in the leather sockets, and stuck out on to the floor.

'It's not worth taking our things upstairs. We must leave ourselves time to dance.'

'We've never danced together,' Anna said.

Yet even in approaching the ballroom Anna noticed there was no music coming from inside.

They opened the doors; and the ballroom—although all the lights were on—was empty.

'The party can't be over,' Don Giovanni said, disconcerted. 'It's not dawn yet.'

'It looks enormous without the people.'

'Perhaps they've all been deceived by the false dawn.'

As she stared into the ballroom, he added:

'There *is* a false dawn. Or perhaps it's only a psychological phenomenon. But just as the sunrise is preceded by the dawn, so the dawn is preceded by something which at least *seems* to make the sky lighter. Or it has been on the few occasions when I've been awake and watching.'

'Occasions', Anna said, 'mostly spent feeling slightly sick in continental trains.' She seemed to give almost the shiver of nausea. 'How *could* Anne face four honeymoons?'

She threw off the shiver, stepped gaily into the ballroom and began to walk straight up the middle.

'We've got it to ourselves,' he said, accompanying her.

'But no music.' She did not look at him but walked as though trying to keep to a straight line.

'Make the chandeliers sing,' he said.

She quickened her steps, so that she drew a little in front of him, still keeping her straight course.

Undeviating, she briefly sang a note.

All the chandeliers responded, neither loud nor soft; the same note but a hint more brazen in its overtones than her voice had been. They sustained their note much longer than she had hers.

Without pausing Anna walked on, emphasising the casualness of what she had done.

The note from the chandeliers died out.

'Do it again,' Don Giovanni said, from behind her. She could tell from his voice that he had halted half way up the ballroom.

'The magic vanishes if the trick is repeated.' She walked

163

straight on, reached the end of the ballroom and stood under the gallery.

'Not all magic,' he said.

She turned to face him. As he came to her, she said:

'I've remembered where all the people must be. In the supper room. Anne said she was going to give them bacon and eggs and champagne.'

'The breakfast room, then.'

'The breakfast room.'

'Are you thinking of wedding breakfasts,' he said, 'which aren't really breakfasts, either?'

'Yes.' She looked at him. 'Of *Anne's* wedding breakfasts.'

They looked away from each other, and both surveyed the ballroom. Its size made them huddle together under the gallery. He put his arm round her waist. They might have been sheltering in a storm.

'Would you like some breakfast?'

'No. Would you?'

'I'm not hungry,' he said.

'I told Anne you didn't eat much. I've just realised why.'

'Why?' he said. 'Why were you telling Anne I didn't eat much?'

'I've just seen it's because Don Giovanni says he needs women more than the bread he eats.'

'Yes, well maybe I do, too,' he said, 'but why were you telling Anne anything about me, whether I eat a lot or a little?'

'O, so she could help me find you.'

'Were you looking for me?'

'Yes.'

'But you'd run away.'

'At first, I thought *you* were looking for *me*. I kept thinking I saw you. Actually, you were in the library the whole time.'

'Do you quite realise what you've confessed to?' he asked.

'I wonder', she said, 'if Don Giovanni's initials influence the use of the keys D and G in the opera?'

'You have a cryptogrammatic mind.'

'I feel at the moment more as if I had no mind. Stay there,' she said, moving his arm from round her and leaving him; 'I want to look down at you from the gallery.'

Dr. Brompius explained to Tom-Tom that although he did not mind eating sandwiches or even a cold buffet supper while he stood up, he had found bacon and eggs digestible only if he ate them sitting down. All the gilt chairs had been removed, once again, from the ballroom to the supper room. But none was vacant. Tom-Tom suggested that Dr. Brompius take his plate up to the small drawing room on the first floor.

When she appeared in the gallery he took up a pose beneath it and sang her, in a pretty baritone, the beginning of Don Giovanni's serenade:

Deh, vieni alla finestra, o mio tesoro!

Deh, vieni a consolar il pianto mio !

'Don't stop,' she said. 'I like your voice.'

'It's all right', he said, 'in an amateur way, like non-vintage wine. But I'm frightened, because of your perfect pitch.'

'I'm sad to inhibit you. That would be perfect bitch.'

'Well in a general way,' he said, 'you don't. And you weren't.'

'No.'

'You do realise, don't you, that you can't simply leave—I mean, go away—at the end of this ball?' He was craning his head upwards, to see her expression in the gallery.

She said nothing.

'Are you', he asked, 'free? I mean, legally?'

'Shush,' she said. 'The people are coming back.'

He looked round. The ballroom doors were open. Two or three figures stood in the doorway, prepared, evidently, to seep back into the ballroom, but for the moment still chattering to people in the hall beyond.

'I wonder', Don Giovanni said, 'if I can do a trick.'

He sprang suddenly, his arm reaching for the bottom of the gallery parapet. But his fingers did not touch it.

'I'm useless as a latin lover,' he said, standing beneath her and dusting his hands together for no reason except that he had failed.

'Come up the stairs,' she said. 'Come quickly.'

'Was that', Ruth asked Edward, 'the first time you've ever done it?'

'Done what? Thrown a snowball? Made a snow-man?'

'Had sex,' she said.

He hesitated.

They were sitting in the back of the car again; under the rug; but not touching each other.

'Well if you want to know, it was,' he said in the end. 'You've got to start somewhere.'

'I suppose people get better at it,' Ruth said, 'with experience.'

'If you didn't enjoy yourself, why blame me? Virgins are notoriously awkward to negotiate.'

'But you were a virgin, too.'

'The word "virgin" only applies to women,' he said.

'It doesn't. I've read it in a book, applied to a man.'

'What book? You don't want to believe everything you see in print.'

'Malory's *Morte D'Arthur*,' Ruth said.

'Did you do it at school?'

'Bits of it. It said Sir Galahad was a virgin.'

'I expect it was a misprint,' Edward said. 'Did the teacher explain it?'

'That wasn't one of the bits we were meant to read. I just read on to that bit for myself.'

'Because you thought it would have something sexy in it?'

'No, because it's literature. It wasn't very interesting.'

'Maybe French literature would be more to the point,' Edward said. 'I wish my French wasn't so bad.'

'But not useless as a lover,' Anna said to him when he joined her in the gallery.

'Are you sure?'

'By the most unmistakable tokens,' she said.

'Well, I think she's a bloody attractive woman,' Edward said as they got out of the car. 'That's why it gave me such satisfaction to throw a snowball at her.'

'That's a contradiction. People throw things at people they *don't* like. I expect it hurt her, too. You'd made it all hard and icy in your hand. And anyway, she wouldn't look at you, even if you do find her attractive.'

'It isn't a contradiction at all,' Edward said. 'That just shews how little you know about sex. And middle-aged women quite often do look at younger men. In France it's part of a young man's education to have a mistress who's rather older than he is, and very experienced.'

'Such as Anna?' Ruth said, challenging him.

'Such as Anna,' he repeated, defying her.

She rushed at him, fighting him.

He put the palms of his hands up, and received hers, like buffers receiving a train. He grasped her wrists and immobilised her hands. But her legs were still free.

She kicked snow at him. Laughing, warmed and rather pleased to be in physical contact with her again, he tried to plant his feet down, wide apart, on her feet, to pin them. He failed. She brought her sharp, white-silk knee up into his crutch.

He pushed her away from him, and doubled up. After a moment he felt his way backwards and sat down on the running-board of the car.

'Christ,' he said. 'Didn't they ever tell you not to kick men there?'

She stood and stared at him, terrified by the mystery and divorce of sex, wondering if it was the same pain as being hit on the breasts or worse.

'You're *ignorant*,' he said.

She became infuriated.

'I don't care if I've——' she angrily began; but he had already disturbed her confidence by questioning her vocabulary; and, not sure of getting the word right, she left the thought unarticulated, turned and ran down the hill and into the house.

'But I can't leap up into galleries,' he said. 'All the women in the world could appear to me on their balconies, and I couldn't get at them.'

'Do you want all the women in the world?'

He thought. Then: 'Yes. But only faintly.'

She laughed.

'If you transferred yourself', she suggested, 'from *Don Giovanni* to *Seraglio*, you could have the help of a ladder.'

'There's no baritone part in *Seraglio*,' he objected. 'And the bass, even supposing I could get down to it, is too buffo for me. I'm essentially serious.'

'Are you?'

'Yes,' he said. 'Yes, I am. You know I am. *Don't* you?'

The door of the supper room stood open, releasing one or two people and a strong, smoked smell of bacon and eggs. Ruth guessed her parents would be in there. She went straight in, sought them out through the crowd, automatically, for reassurance, like a puppy, almost by nose or tactile sense: but once she had found them she did not want them.

'Hullo, dear,' Myra said. 'Where's Edward?'

'Outside, as far as I know. He wanted some air.'

'He's not drunk, is he?' Myra asked.

'Not so's he can't stand up,' Ruth replied, and drifted away from her parents into the crowd. Her answer, although it shewed a sophisticated refusal to be impressed by the idea of drunkenness, displeased her as much as if it had been a weak answer, because she knew that what had brought it to her mind was the fact that, when she had last seen him, Edward could not stand up.

As Ruth disappeared into the crowd, Myra said to Rudy: 'O dear. I do hope she's going to get something to eat.'

'Now don't fuss, Mother. She won't come to any harm

if she goes without her breakfast for once. She looks over-grown to me as it is.'

'They grow up so quickly these days,' Myra said. 'It's these sexy advertisements they see all over the place.'

Anna stood leaning her full weight on the parapet, look-ing down into the ballroom, where still only a sprinkling of people had appeared. Don Giovanni stood with an arm loosely and comfortably thrown round her, like a cloak or the wing of a man-high bird, while he looked down on the top of her head.

'As I seem to have spent all evening telling you,' he said lazily into her hair and the black lace at the back of it, 'it's no *use* running away. Because you don't want to.'

She did not contradict.

'If you could keep imagining you saw me at this ball,' he said, 'just think what you'd be like at Piccadilly Circus in the rush hour.'

She still did not contradict.

'Besides,' he added. 'From a purely practical point of view . . .'

'What?' she asked.

'Well you must realise, if you think about it. I can quite easily find out who you are, where you live, all about you—from Tom-Tom.'

She stirred away from him and began to object, but he counter-objected:

'All right, so you wouldn't answer my letters or speak to me on the phone. But I can get Tom-Tom to invite us both to dinner. He'd do it for me. He's got a soft spot for me.'

She moved quite away from him, turned deliberately towards him and spoke contemptuously.

'You talk as if you were his valet. You *boast* of his soft spot for you.'

'All right,' he said, challengingly. 'I'm not his valet, but I am his hireling. So what? I'm not ashamed of it. It doesn't *matter*.'

'O my dear,' she said. 'Before you boast of having your master's ear, have you considered *my* position in this house?'

'What do you mean?'

'I've only to tell Anne not to dream of inviting us both to dinner. I've only to tell Anne to tell Tom-Tom *not* to tell you my name.'

'All right,' he said, submissively this time, after a moment, and bowed his head. 'All the same,' he said, raising it again. 'You really want—'

'Oh, want,' she said, disparagingly.

'Why must you be so withering? It was you that said that in this house the servants' staircase was appropriate to us. Now you talk as if you belonged to *their* class.'

'I do in a way,' she said wearily. 'I married into it;

'Did you?'

'That's how I know them.'

'Them?' he said quickly. 'Which of them? They've only been married a short time themselves.'

'O, Anne, of course,' she said. 'I've told you, I hardly know Tom-Tom.' She began slowly: 'My husband was——'

'Was? But he isn't dead?'

'No. I said "was" to try and get the time sequence right for you. My husband was Anne's———'

'Let me guess,' he interposed. 'Anne's brother?'

'No, that would be "is", I suppose,' Anna said. 'He presumably still would be her brother. . .' She looked at Don Giovanni, with a gentler expression. 'My dear, you grope through my labyrinth amazingly well. You don't get it *right*, but my God you get the feel of the thing.'

'Well, tell me, then,' he said.

'My husband was Anne's first husband. She married him. She divorced him. I married him. I divorced him.'

'O,' Don Giovanni said; then, evidently re-treading the old while he became accustomed to the new information: 'And now he lives abroad?'

'Mm.'

'Well I can't think', Don Giovanni said, coming to it finally, 'why you didn't tell me before. It's not monstrous. It's not incestuous. It's just that you and Anne have a husband in common. That's all.'

'That's all,' she agreed. 'I didn't tell you because I thought it might mislead you. I thought you might think it explained everything—or at least things it doesn't.'

'What an odd relationship you must have with Anne,' he said.

'There you go, you see . . . I haven't. What do you think? Do you think we discuss him, exchange the confidences of the marriage bed?'

'No. No, I don't.'

'Then do you think we avoid the subject? Do you think it's the one subject that's never mentioned between us?'

'Well, more, I should have guessed, in that direction than the other.'

'It isn't so,' she said, her voice very tired. 'That's the extraordinary thing. It isn't an extraordinary relationship at all. The really strange thing is that I think it never comes into either of our minds. I think we've both simply *forgotten* what it was that brought us together.'

Sitting on the running board, Edward became quite numb with cold and knew that, having exaggerated his injury to Ruth, he was now exaggerating it to himself. As a matter of fact, he had been bearing down so hard on her hands that her legs had not had much freedom of man-oeuvre and she had not got in a very forceful blow. Never-theless he felt justified in his exaggeration, because she *might* have injured him badly: she was ignorant enough: by which he meant that she needed a lesson.

He got up and trudged round in the snow, trying to remember to stamp his feet to warm them up. He did not stir far from the Blumenbaums' car: it was in his mind that if a policeman should come on him loitering beside the cars of people who did not know him and would not speak up for him he might be arrested.

The back of the Blumenbaums' car rose, and to some height, not quite vertically but at the staidest of inclines, like the back of a spinster on a bicycle. Edward's own taste preferred cars that crouched low as though over dropped handlebars. That was what he would have bought if he had had the same amount of money to spend on a car as Rudy Blumenbaum had spent on this. But he did not trust his own taste, and thought that, if he had had the money to spend, he would merely have betrayed the shallowness of his taste. He believed in good and bad taste as absolutes, though not in his own ability to tell them apart. What Rudy had got for his money was not merely luxury but respectable luxury: the respectability that went with old-fashioned things, with the look of ancien régime. Edward hated and despised Rudy Blumen-baum's car but would not for the world have forfeited his connexion with it: he half hoped a policeman *would* challenge him: it was a connexion to an object Edward could not have acquired, because his taste would not have been elastic enough to let him reach for it. He felt towards the Blumenbaums' car as a young man might to an elderly spinster distant connexion who was tiresome, old-fashioned and tedious in her insistence on discipline—her hints that young people should be taught to sit up straight by having boards strapped to their backs—and yet invaluable because she had a title.

On the staidly sloping back of the car snow had uncertainly gathered—it might all slide off, in a sheet, at any moment: it had compiled from the bottom upwards, and at the edges and top the staid dark green paint was still visible. Taking great care not to dislodge the whole sheet, Edward's finger wrote in the snow 'JEWBOY'; and then he went, quite happily, back to the ball.

Twenty or thirty people were now in the ballroom promenading. There was still no music, though one or two members of the band had come back and were re-establishing themselves on the platform. There was, however, an air of altered purpose about them—an unhappy air. They had set up music stands and were propping music sheets on them, as though they were going to play real music.

Don Giovanni said to Anna, in the gallery:

'It doesn't alter anything. We come back to the fact that you can't run away because you don't want to. A person of your temperament can't want to.'

'Why?' she asked. 'Why shouldn't I?'

'Because to part is to die a little. The remark', he added, 'of a rather well-read hairdresser. I'm sorry,' he superadded. 'When I'm very tired I start laying double-yolked puns.'

She laughed. 'We could both do with a good day's sleep,' she said.

'Well shall you have it at my flat, or I at yours?'

'If there were no other', she said, 'there are practical objections. I can't be seen simply going off with you.'

'Why not? What would it matter? But anyway, even if you want to observe the proprieties, it's perfectly all right. You're forgetting it'll be morning. It's perfectly all right to be seen going anywhere with anyone in the morning. It's as safe as going home with the milkman.'

'Had you ever thought about the milkman?' she asked sleepily. 'Did you know about the place he occupies in our civilisation? He's a super-parent-figure.'

'I can see', Don Giovanni said, 'that he's a sort of daily Santa Claus.'

'He dates, in one's memory', Anna said, 'from before that awful moment of divorce when one realises one has to have *two* parents, one of each sex. That is, he's a man: yet one gets milk from him.'

'That's so absurd', Don Giovanni said, 'that I think it must be true. Or else I'm *very* tired.'

Looking into the ballroom Anna distinguished, among the promenaders, the man who looked like a boiled egg.

Trying, with fatigued systematicness, all the doors in turn on the first floor, Anne looked in at the little music room where she sometimes played the piano while Anna sang. But Anna was not there. It was a practical room, almost the only practical room in the house: its single ornament was a large crystal egg, the size of an ostrich egg, which lay in the middle of the mantelpiece with a screw of silver paper pushed under its edge to prevent it from rolling off.

Although Anna was not there, Anne went in and shut the door. She rolled up her lamé skirt and tried to make her suspender tighter.

The egg on the mantel always reminded her of Leda. She liked pictures of Leda and the swan: Correggio's, the Leonardo composition, anyone's, indeed, that she could think of—she admitted that it was not the treatment but the subject itself which pleased her. It gave her, as a matter of fact, an erotic thrill. She decided to remember to ask Anna, when she should find her, to explain the psychology of the thrill. She herself could not account for it, because she had never felt the least desire to copulate with a swan.

She carefully rolled down the lamé and took a step, but found that the suspender was no tighter.

It came into her mind that when Tom-Tom was dressed for sailing his thick feet in gum boots or waders resembled the strong, grey-black, waterproof feet of a wading bird.

'My eye has been lighting on that funny little man all night,' Anna said.

'Which one?'

'With the chinese waistcoat and the paunch.'

'Who is he?'

'I've no idea. Neither in real life nor in costume. Nobody seems to have any idea. He's always alone.'

'He doesn't really look like anyone. Neither in real life nor in costume.'

'Perhaps he's done a rather brilliant thing', Anna suggested, 'and come as an anonymous eighteenth-century man. Anyway, he reminds me of a boiled egg.'

'By the way,' Don Giovanni said. 'About the milkman. You realise he also lays eggs on one's doorstep?'

'Leda,' they both said.

'Have you noticed', Don Giovanni said, 'that the beginning of love always is to find the same thought in the other person's mind?'

'O, love,' she said, dismissively.

'You *can't* be so offhand . . .' he said.

'It's curious,' Anna said. 'Your Walter Pater incantation about Leda is one of Anne's favourite quotations, too.'

Edward found Ruth straight away, went straight up to her and put his arm round her waist.

'Are you all right?' she asked instantly, breathlessly. She wanted, curious, but embarrassed at being curious, to look down at the lower half of his body, which in the tight-fitting breeches would be, she felt, almost naked to her scrutiny; in her anxiety not to look down, she fixed her eyes on his face, with a disingenuous concentration, as though his lower limbs were an acquaintance she was trying not to see walk past in the street.

'I'm fine,' he replied, having forgotten why he should not be. 'Why? I'm feeling dandy.'

'*Are* you?' Ruth said, distrustfully, drawing away from him a little. 'Why?'

'I've been thinking,' he said. 'It *is* rather magnificent, isn't it? I mean, the first time one has it—to have it in a Bentley.'

'Anne divorced him', Don Giovanni said, making a resumé, 'and then you divorced him. And then Anne married again.'

'And again. And again . . .' Anna said, a touch wryly, a touch wearily.

'But not you?'

'No. I didn't.'

'But you had plenty of lovers?'

'Oh, what's "plenty"?' she said, mocking him. 'What are your standards? By Messalina's standards, I'd make a poor shewing.'

'Well, enough, then,' he emended.

'Enough? Yes, enough. It isn't hard, you know, just to find *men*. I am—or I have been—quite attractive.'

'Do you imagine you have to tell me that?'

'Well I've let you in, you know, to my imperfections.'

'But I'm one of the people', he said, 'who do prefer life to perfection.'

'You're too innocent, Rudy,' Myra Blumenbaum said, as they walked towards the ballroom. 'I'm sure he kisses her when they're alone together. O dear,' she added, 'I never meant us to stay so late. It must be almost dawn already.'

'O go on,' he said. 'The kids've got to have their fun.'

'Don't you *mind* if he kisses her?'

'I didn't mean that. I meant we've got to stay up a bit for once, to give them a chance. I don't expect he does kiss her.'

'I'm sure he does. They're all so precocious nowadays.'

'Perhaps I'd better have a word with young Edward.'

'O no, *don't,* Rudy. What would you say?'

'O, you know me,' Rudy said. 'Mild as milk when it comes to it. I expect I'd just say "Steady, Eddy".'

The band began to play: but it was music of a kind to which neither musicians nor dancers were accustomed.

'O dear,' Anna said, half laughing into Don Giovanni's arm, which she was holding. 'Now we shall never dance together. Why are eighteenth-century dances so *lugubrious*? The last thing one could do is *dance* to them.'

'Not for nothing are so many of them called contredanses.'

'I expect they're really for funerals. It's all a misunderstanding. Dr. Brompius arranged these, by the way. They're by Swedish court composers.'

'They sound it,' he lugubriously replied.

Nevertheless, a few people down in the ballroom were trying to dance to them. They had arranged themselves in two lines, and were trying to improvise a dance on the model of the statelier kind of country dance. But it was obvious that no one could remember the model. The two lines became straggly, the dancers at the edges dropping out and joining the crowd which was still occupying most of the ballroom as a promenade.

The musicians played as though they, too, would like the opportunity to drop out.

Dr. Brompius had not been able to arrange a part for the man who had made the bean-bag noise. The man was on the platform, but doing nothing; on the verge of sleep.

Anna's eye was drawn to the tall elegant windows of the ballroom. The sky outside had become a lighter grey.

'Is it the dawn?' she asked Don Giovanni. 'Or just the false dawn?'

They both watched for a moment. The light increased perceptibly: then unmistakably.

'Dawn,' he said, his voice depressed.

Grey bars of cloud stretched across the window: straggling, flocky, coming to pieces at the edges: just like the bars of dancers across the floor.

On the ceiling, the lights were negated by the light from outside. They continued to shine, but like a person talking without an audience. They were hardly lights any more; their illumination ceased to illuminate and took on colour; they were mere yellow things, pale yellow, easily overlooked. They could no longer strike any fire from the chandeliers, whose nimbus shrank to a mere slight fizziness, the colour of champagne; each chandelier was like a badly bleached, badly coiffured blonde head, the bleach and the set growing—straggling—out.

Perhaps dawn brought a momentary thaw; perhaps it was the first sign of a general thaw: outside in the cul-de-sac a little furry inch of snow, like a caterpillar, fell from one of the thin branches low down on one of the trees. After a minute, the snow began falling off the whole length of the branch. The first consignment landed, exploded and then lay opened out like a tassel on top of the torso of the snow-man Edward had made. The rest fell straight and whole, a diagonal whiplash, across the roof of Rudy Blumenbaum's car. The very end of the line of snow, representing the very tip of the branch it had tumbled off, struck the top corner of the sloping back of the car. The snow piled on the back was set shifting. After a second's hesitation it was all dislodged and carried away, crumpling on to the road somewhere behind the car's rear bumper.

Two doors along from the music room, in the small drawing room, Anne found Dr. Brompius. He was sitting on the plump, pretty, flowered sofa; on the empty square next to him lay a coldly greasy plate.

He stood up as Anne came in; and simultaneously she asked:

'Dr. Brompius, have you seen Anna?'

and he asked:

'Madame, it is time for the Swedish dance suites?'

Dismayed by having forgotten, and dismayed again by her own liquid hypocrisy, Anne said:

'That's why I'm looking for Anna. She'd be so disappointed to miss them.'

'Then I expect she will already be down there. Shall we go, madame?'

'Dr. Brompius, you go,' Anne said, as though asking him a confidential favour. She moved his plate on to the top of a pretty little walnut escritoire which stood against the wall, and sat down in its place on the sofa. 'I'm so exhausted, I must just have a moment's rest on my own.'

'I understand,' he replied, and to her surprise began to withdraw. From the door, he said:

'I have not seen the lady you asked after for many hours. She went away with a gentleman in the character of Don Giovanni.'

'Are you sure?' Anne cried after him, half rising from the sofa. 'In black? With a mask on?'

'Yes, yes, yes,' Dr. Brompius said: in the corridor he had heard the Swedish music from below, and was hurrying away to it.

Anne sat back in the sofa, contented: so contented that

she presently reached up and, from where she sat, contrived to get her fingertips to grip on the ridge of the pulldown of the escritoire. She pulled it down and revealed, inside, an intricate wooden simulation of the façade of a Grecian temple. Heaving a little over the arm of the sofa, she got her hand to penetrate the peristyle, and it came out tugging after it a pretty little George II silver basket, in which Anne always kept a few peppermint creams.

'There's Dr. Lugubrius himself,' Don Giovanni said, pointing down into the ballroom. 'He's just come in. He wants to listen.'

They watched the top of his head as he swam forcefully through the crowd and took up a position near the band—who noticed him, pretended not to, and were obviously made uneasy by him.

'There's your boiled egg, too,' Don Giovanni said. 'He's arrived in time for breakfast.'

He was walking, alone, in the crowd.

The ballroom was almost all crowd now, with only a little dancing going on in the middle. The dancers were almost wholly engulfed by the promenaders, like its prey by an amoeba.

'You *can't* leave me,' Don Giovanni said to Anna.

'Why *can't* I? Because I'm one of your victims?' But there was hardly any challenge left in her voice.

'Because I'm one of yours. I love you.'

'O, love,' she said, in the same disparaging tone in which she had said it before; but with less fire.

'You *can't* write it off like that.'

'Why can't I?' But her voice was almost wholly worn out.

'Because you believe in it,' he said. 'I almost said "believe in *him*".'

16

His statue stood in the niche on the landing at the top of the grand staircase, so that he presided over the house.

Anna had once pointed out to Anne that he presided in the same way over Mozart's operas. Anne's mind often ran with Mozart quotations, and espccially so when she thought about Anna—whose mind, she knew, teemed with them. Anne's own store had supplied the memory of Pedrillo invoking Cupid as a heart-thief—Nun Cupido, du Herzensdieb—and bidding him hold the ladder down which the women were to be thieved away from the seraglio; and the memory of Countess Almaviva praying to Cupid in the direct character of Love when she sang

Porgi, Amor . . .

And Cherubino himself, Anne now added, passing the statue on her way to the stairs, was first cousin to Cupid.

She thought, as she descended, of the two as infant cousins playing together like Leonardo's Christ and John the Baptist; or as closer than cousins, like Leonardo's other two little boys, playing together after emerging from a single shell, from Leda's double-yolked egg.

Anne turned, and went some way back up the stairs to look at the statue.

Seen at close quarters, he was hideous. Partly, of course, it was his age: an infant aged at least two hundred years—in the wood, that was to say; aged two millennia, probably, in the mythological conception. His gold was peeling off in great leaves, as though he had got sunburn, shewing the crimson ground beneath; his wing was chipped; worm had visited, and then left, him. But he *was* hideous, also, in the mythological conception, and all the restoration in the world could not have hidden it. A great lump, over-fed, overgrown, over-active for his presumptive age, if you judged his age by his chubbiness, he should hardly have been able to crawl: yet here he was, flying about the world, a precocious monster, and already thinking of nothing except sex. Able to fly and yet uncertain about alighting, he had landed with one spreading, stubby toe on the ground. But his airy pose of being poised little became him, since he had in reality to be propped up on a rusty iron stanchion which rose from his plinth and disappeared into his nether world, into the flutter of wooden drapery which he daintily kept round his pubic region, with the indelicate coyness of an old man wrapping himself up in a bathing towel and yet not scrupling to reveal the far more indelicate swag of his corpulent belly. Cupid, corpulent as any old man about the belly, peevish about the mouth, petulant in the cheeks, puffed up and actually worm-riddled in the buttocks, had no business to cover his nakedness, since he was still only an infant, matter for old women to bath: Anne would have bathed him, if she had not thought his gold would peel wholly off: though in fact it was for his own mother, from whom he never strayed far for all his pretences to independence of mischief making, to keep the fat child kempt, if she—that woman, that goddess—had not been a slut and a whore, her mind on other things. In any case, there was no purpose in his fluttering drapery, since the whole of him was phallic. He was phallic to his wing tips (the chip off the end of one of them could not disguise or impair it): phallic to his fat tiptoe: phallic to his arrow tips, (If he had ever managed to complete the action his carver had given him to have perpetually begun, if he had managed to pull out the arrow he was just fingering in the quiver and had got it notched to the —now vanished—bow string, his shot would have lethally penetrated straight to the heart of the ballroom,) Even the base of his quiver, a little depository of weapons which he wore at loins height, made a socket like a scrotum. So it was no good his veiling his mystery from women, his precocious potency from men, teasing maidens to guess what was there and young men maidens to guess what should be done with it.

He was quite hideous, seen from close to.

Anne wished for a world in which all weapons were only phallic symbols: in which the stroke of death should be not merely *as* but wholly and solely a lover's pinch.

Standing in front of the statue she said, audibly, a prayer to the only god she believed in: but him she believed capable of saving the world.

'O Cupid, save the world.'

17

From the gallery Anna saw Anne come energetically into the ballroom—or at least, Anna detected, with a resolution to be energetic—fall on her guests and drive them into dancing to the funereal music. Head down, she bustled, a plump and indomitable little Pallas Athena armoured in lamé (Queen Anne in an heroical allegory) or perhaps Pallas Athena's downy little owl, to the rescue of a battle line that was certainly breaking if not broken. Anna wondered if her willingness to sacrifice the last vestige of her energy to saving Dr. Brompius's face was prompted by remorse at having, earlier, sacrificed her friend by pushing her into his maw. Anne rallied the line that existed or was hanging on to existence; she drummed up new recruits; she had got both Voltaire and Rudy Blumenbaum, one by each hand, and was dragging them, and with them a whole wilting row, forward to meet another row—most of whom had not come forward at the right moment: to bow: to retreat again. It was a slow and stately version of nuts-in-may. On the ebb Anne retreated with so much stately energy, bumping her back so strenuously into those of the crowd who got in her way, that the crowd was obliged to yield, even to make space for the dancing which, it was now forced to notice, was taking place in the middle of it

Then suddenly, at the moment when the thing might have worked, everything stopped because the man who looked like a boiled egg fell to the floor in the middle of the crowd in the middle of the ballroom.

'Your egg's fainted,' Don Giovanni said.

Voltaire—and Anne, of course, too—were promptly there. People stopped talking. Anna heard Voltaire say, kneeling beside the man:

'These eighteenth-century clothes are too tight. I'll see if I can get it undone.'

The musicians, uncertain what had happened, took the opportunity to stop playing the difficult music and lean forward to find out.

Anna noticed that Ruth Blumenbaum's young man, the one dressed as Casanova, was also there, kneeling.

Voltaire mouthed something, evidently meant for only Anne to read; but of course other people took it up and queried it—including the young Casanova, who queried it and evidently received confirmation because he suddenly, as though in horror, removed the hand he was leaning on from its proximity to the man like a boiled egg.

Only Dr. Brompius neither understood nor attended. Standing beside the platform he endlessly remonstrated— Anna could see but not hear, because the whole room had begun to talk—with the silent musicians. They ignored him. But he went on. At last one of the musicians sitting near the outside of the platform felt obliged to remonstrate back, to expostulate, with a touch of self-righteousness, almost, in his exasperation, and finally to—in a gesture which seemed to fling Dr. Brompius's unreasonableness down for all to see—point: and thus bring it to Dr. Brompius's attention that in the centre of the ballroom a man lay dead.

18

Anna hurtled down the stairs. Don Giovanni, following her for his life, felt something sticky detain the sole of his shoe. He tried to kick it off, did not succeed and had to pause for a second because he was afraid it was going to pull his shoe off altogether. It was a small white lump, dirtily grained with black marks. It might have been snow, brought in from the street, soiled by tyres. But it stuck. He peeled it off, noticing that it was a peppermint cream that had been trodden, moved a little further on and then discarded by a hundred other soles; he flung it away; and ran violently after Anna, who said:

'Don't try to stop me. I've got to go to Anne.'

'I'm not trying to stop you. I'm only trying to come with you.'

But at the entrance to the ballroom they threw themselves against a hundred backs.

It was obviously impossible to make any penetration.

'It would be more help to Anne if we started a movement for going home.'

'Yes,' Anna said. 'I will.'

In the portico, he said:

'You can't be so cruel.'

'Only to myself,' she said.

He followed rather than accompanied her up the little hill out of the cul-de-sac, because she had already cast him off, leaving him to trail behind like an urchin offering services that were not wanted.

A cab came past almost as soon as she turned into the main road, and she stopped it.

Even so, he hung about, as though hoping to pick up something she might fling to him.

'Go straight ahead,' she said to the driver. 'I'll tell you the address in a moment.'

Presently, looking out of the taxi window, she noticed that the snow in the streets was already stained brownish, perhaps melting. She neither hoped nor did not hope that it would survive the day.

The next time she looked out it was because the taxi was taking her along a narrow street she liked: two low brick terraces, grey in this cold light, built as cottages but now expensive.

The taxi turned a corner. Anna saw the driver's head duck for a second, and her own eyes winced. The sunrise was spread in bars across the sky in front of them: hideous crimson and blood-coloured bars, like the elements of a monstrous electric fire aping the cosiness of coal.

She tipped the driver enough to make him flatter her with the word Miss.

'Good night, Miss. Or should I say Good morning?'

'Either way,' Anna said, completely coldly, 'a hideous time of day.'

He was confounded. Not till she had her key in the lock did he call out:

'Anyway. Happy new year.'

She let herself in, thinking about death.